Three-Zee on a Horse

John A. Miller, Jr.

[The seventh 3Z story]

Tragedy strikes a mother and her little boy when their car rolls down a steep embankment and catches fire while upside down in a creek. Meanwhile, their carjacker disappears into the Pocono Mountains forest adjacent to the Mountain Woods Resort. Three-Zee Zook discovers the bodies and, with her best friend, Bambi Bamberger, goes searching for the carjacker after the ghosts of the woman and her son show up almost on their doorstep. Things get complicated when the woman's mob-connected husband and father arrive at the resort and immediately lock horns with one of the resort owners, a clone of Ebenezer Scrooge. Then there's the new girl in town, wrangler for the resort's new stable and small herd of riding horses. Both Three-Zee and Bambi can ride, but Three-Zee discovers that being dragged by a horse with her foot caught in a stirrup and her head bouncing along the ground can have some serious repercussions.

Other books in the *Three-Zee* series:

(1) *Three-Zee*

(2) *Three-Zee at the Beach*

(3) *Three-Zee in the Mountains*

(4) *Three-Zee in a Dilemma*

(5) *Three-Zee at a Wedding*

(6) *Three-Zee in a Maze*

Three-Zee on a Horse

John A. Miller, Jr.

This is a work of fiction. Except for actual historical figures, any resemblance between any character in this story and any person living or dead is purely coincidental.

Dedication

To Amorette Anderson, an accomplished author in her own right, who's been there to help encourage me when I get bogged down while writing this series.

Acknowledgment

Cover photo by Barbara Olsen.

Catastrophe

With terror in her eyes, the woman looked out the passenger side window, a window she'd lowered when the man outside at the traffic light pressed a handgun against it. "Please, let me and my little boy go."

"I don't care about you or your damned kid, but I do kind of like your wheels. Yeah, I've always wanted a Beemer. My old man did, too, but he never was able to afford one, so this'll put me one up on him."

The driver reached for her door handle, but the man outside, still pointing his gun at her head, snapped, "No, stay in the car. You're going to drive me. The kid's trapped in that car seat, so he won't be a problem, and if you give me any crap, well, either he won't have a mom, or you won't have a kid, or both. Now, hit that unlock button or you die."

As soon as the lock clicked, the man outside yanked the door open, jumped inside, and slammed the door shut. Meanwhile, the little boy in the car seat, probably no more than three, started crying and then screaming.

"Shut that damned kid up, or I'll shut him up." The man twisted around in his seat and pointed the gun at the boy.

"Johnny, please stop crying. Mommy's okay," the woman said. She breathed a sigh of relief when the boy stopped screaming and toned down to a whimper. "Okay, now what," she asked the man who had once again pointed the gun at her head.

"Get us out of this damned town. Then maybe I'll let you and the kid go, or maybe not."

The woman looked at the lights of the minimarket on the corner, so near and yet so far. The store was open twenty-four hours, but at this late hour nobody was in the parking lot, nobody was filling up at the gas pumps, and there were no other cars in the road. She probably could have driven into the lot, but with nobody around, the man could easily shoot her, push her body out of the car, and drive away before the store clerk could get outside to investigate the noise, assuming the clerk didn't merely hide inside and maybe call 911.

"Okay, I'll go where you want, but please let us out then. You can have the car, and I promise I won't call the cops right away."

"Yeah, right. Shut up and drive."

The light was green, so the woman drove straight ahead, trying to drive carefully to avoid being spotted by a police patrol car. Before the cops would be able to pull her over, she was pretty sure her unwanted passenger would shoot her or her son. Either was unthinkable.

"Turn right here," the man said. She followed his orders and turned onto a narrower, but still paved, road.

"Where are we going?"

"None of your damned business, so shut up and drive."

The woman glanced to her right. Her captor looked to be in his mid-twenties and clean-shaven with rather long sandy hair. In all he was fairly nondescript, and in the dim light from the car's interior displays she couldn't see any particular identifiable markings, especially as the winding road required her to keep her attention mostly focused on where she was going to avoid driving into a ditch.

The man noticed her looking at him. "Pay attention to where you're going. I don't want to wind up in a hospital bed."

She resisted the urge to tell him she'd rather he wound up in a morgue, figuring he'd probably take it badly.

"There's a dirt road off to the left about a half-mile ahead. Turn into it."

The woman nodded.

Suddenly a deer burst out of the trees to the left. She swerved to avoid it, tried to correct when she realized she was going to go off the road to the left, overcorrected, and flipped over the guard rail on the right, crashing down a steep embankment. The car tumbled, rolling over and over several times until it came to rest upside down in a creek at the base of a much higher rocky embankment, one that appeared to be man-made.

About halfway down the hill the man, who hadn't been wearing his seatbelt, was tossed free. He landed on a grassy patch, tumbled a few times, and then lay silent. The woman and little boy were less fortunate because the creek wasn't deep enough to prevent the wreckage from catching fire. The woman was already dead, her head crushed by the collapsing roof, but her little boy screamed in the back seat, trapped in his child seat. Then the gas tank exploded, and all was silent except for the gurgling of the brook, the crackling of the flames, and eventually, the chirping of a few nocturnal birds. A few sparks from the wreckage landed in the surrounding grass and weeds, but the grass was still wet from a recent heavy shower, so the few small blazes the sparks ignited quickly went out.

Eventually, the man regained consciousness, sat up, and stared at the still-flaming wreck below. After uttering a few choice remarks, he staggered to his feet and struggled up the hill to the road. He looked around to try to figure out where he was, crossed the road, and limped into the trees.

The road was little traveled, especially so early in the morning, so no vehicle passed by until the flames on the wreckage had died down so far as to be unnoticeable.

A New Career?

I looked across the living room at Bambi. "Do you think I should become a PI?"

"A P-what?" Pete said.

"Shut up, Pete. I was talking to Bambi."

Bambi looked up from her phone. I guess she was checking her email or texting somebody or scrolling through Facebook or Instagram or Twitter or TikTok or, well, you get the idea, but she hadn't been paying attention to me. "Three-Zee, what did you say?"

"I asked whether you think I should become a PI?"

"A PI? Oh, a private investigator. No, probably not."

"Why not? I mean, I've investigated I don't know how many murders, and I have an inside track because I can interrogate their ghosts."

"No, for a couple of reasons. Number one, the ghosts have never been much help in identifying their killers. Number two, you've investigated the murders, true, but mostly you've stumbled upon the killers by sheer dumb luck. Besides, you have your job here to consider."

"Yeah, there is that, actually all of that."

"Definitely all of that and then some," Pete added. "Maybe if you and the little deer went in together…"

Bambi glared at him. "I'm out, definitely out. Chef at a fancy restaurant earning at least six figures is my goal."

I choked, but Pete smiled and said, "That's a noble goal, Bambi, and I'm sure you'll get there, darling." I choked again.

"Well, we haven't had any murders or even suspicious deaths in the area since last fall," I admitted, "so you're probably right in that I wouldn't be able to make enough money in fees to support myself."

"Of course, PIs make most of their income tracking down errant spouses or finding lost dogs or whatever," Pete said.

"Which really isn't exciting. I guess I'll have to stick with being Assistant Activities Director for a while longer."

"Yeah, do something within your skill set."

"Shut up, Pete!"

** ** **

My name is Zelanie Zephora Zook. Fortunately, my friends have abbreviated that godawful mess to Three-Zee. I'm nearly thirty years old, still unmarried, and drop-dead gorgeous. (Shut up, Pete!)

Pete actually *is* drop-dead gorgeous—Can you use that term to describe a guy?—but his major flaw is he's actually dead, a ghost. Stepson of George Wylie, the manager and part owner of the Mountain Woods

Resort in the Pocono Mountains of eastern Pennsylvania where Bambi and I labor for our daily bread—and pizza, and wine, and, but I digress…—Pete was shot to death in the resort's grounds a couple of years ago. Since then, unlike most ghosts who move on after learning how and why they died, Pete has hung around. His reason: Bambi.

Bambi is Bambi Bamberger, my best friend, who, as mentioned above, is training to be a chef in the resort's kitchens while also filling in as a part-time front desk clerk. Until last summer Bambi couldn't even see or hear Pete although they had somehow developed a relationship, something about that exciting chill. For some unknown reason, now she can see and hear him, and the relationship is still going strong.

You may suspect from my comments that I can see and hear Pete, too. Fortunately, or maybe unfortunately depending upon your point of view, I can see and hear most ghosts, excepting of course those who've moved on to wherever. Ghosts can make themselves invisible to we mortals who can see them, but that's their choice.

One of my regular chores as Assistant Activities Director is to lead hikes of adventurous guests around the vast woodlands that cover most of our property. Okay, they're not exactly vast, but they're big enough, and you have to consider that part of the property is a big, man-made lake and a cluster of buildings including a big lodge for guests, indoor and outdoor pools, residences for live-in employees, of whom there are quite a few, and plenty of parking. Bambi and I, and Pete although he doesn't exactly require living accommodations, share a small one-bedroom cottage that isn't deemed of adequate quality for the paying guests. Most other employees live in a big dormitory building that also contains George's apartment. Under construction adjacent to all of the above is a stable for the horses for horseback riding, which is coming soon. Meanwhile, we walk, or we row boats, canoes, or kayaks in season, like when the lake isn't frozen over or harboring penguins and walruses.

A favorite hike, especially now that a footbridge has been constructed over the spillway beside the dam, is the lakeside trail that goes completely around the lake, a walk of almost two-and-a-half miles. Until the bridge was built, we could hike across the top of the dam, but the spillway was way too dangerous to try to cross on foot. Of course, when I first began working at Mountain Woods, now about two-and-a-half years ago, the resort didn't own the entire perimeter of the lake. A wedge of land containing a feeder stream and a large pond on that stream was owned by a particularly nasty old man named Abner Whitelaw. Abner is currently serving a long sentence in one of the state's less-than-luxurious accommodations, and the resort has purchased his land.

This morning I was scheduled to lead a lakeside trail hike, and I had twelve guests signed up, a goodly number. Many guests come to totally relax, utilizing the pools, the spa, the dining room—full American plan with all meals included—and the lounge—booze not included—hey, we have to make a profit somewhere—but others like to get in their exercise.

At nine o'clock we set off on our clockwise trek. I usually allowed at least two hours because the hikers would stop to admire the scenery, snap pictures with their phones, admire the birds and beasts, text pictures from their phones to their friends, stand in awe on top of the dam, post pictures from their phones on multiple social media accounts, admire the new footbridge, text more pictures… well, you get the idea. Anyway, by leaving at nine we were pretty much assured of being back to the main lodge before noon, where the hikers could stoke their metabolisms and replace all those lost calories by partaking of the massive buffet. (I got to eat in the employee dining room; not nearly as massive or gourmet, but edible and included.)

We had just rounded the end of one of the coves that the trail bordered, me bringing up the rear, when I saw it. At first, I thought it was a couple of piles of charred wood, one about five feet long and a foot or so high and the other about half that size. However, even though the two piles lay right beside the trail, none of the other hikers paid the least bit of attention to them. When I reached the piles, I realized that they weren't wood. They were charred human remains, one an adult and one probably a young child. I'm not usually queasy, and I've seen more than my share of deceased people, but none I'd ever seen was that bad. I had to turn and empty the contents of my stomach, two cups of coffee and one piece of dry toast, into the weeds beside the trail. The last hiker in line came running back to me and asked whether I was all right. I explained I must have eaten something that hadn't agreed with me, and then the two of us hurried to join up with the others.

Besides being able to see and talk with ghosts, which are really quite normal looking except for the fact they're dead, I sometimes get these visions of the deceased as they looked at the time they died, not necessarily a pleasant sight. This one certainly wasn't, and I was doubly sure of what I'd just seen when I looked back and the two burnt corpses had disappeared.

One problem with these visions is they don't provide precise information as to where the bodies are located although they've always been within a couple of miles. Consequently, I pretty much knew there were two burnt bodies, an adult and a child, somewhere nearby. There was a good chance their ghosts would show up in the near future, but I'd have to wait for that. This was the first time I'd had to deal with a child, and I wasn't sure how well I'd be able to handle it.

The Damn Dam

We made it to the top of the dam, a massive earth-fill structure that slopes down about ten feet to the water on the lake side and about fifty or sixty feet on the other. The outflow is a fairly wide creek at the bottom of that slope, and then the land slopes up again rather steeply to a road. I always paused the hike on top of the dam, which is at least fifteen or twenty feet wide with a number of large rocks that can be used as seats. I had just settled my butt on one of the rocks when a young woman yelled for me to join her.

"What's wrong?" I asked as I approached the spot where she was looking down the long slope to the outflow.

"There's something down there in the creek. It looks something like an overturned car."

"That's odd. I've never seen anything in the creek before." I reached the edge and looked down. The slope is fairly steep and covered with rocks, mostly the size of a bowling ball or maybe a bit larger, but it is walkable if one is careful. There definitely was something in the creek that could be a car or at least the underside of one.

Maybe I should learn not to investigate such things, but I suppose I at least have a private eye instinct if not the skill or license. Anyway, I immediately began working my way down the dam face, trying not to stumble and face plant in some rather sharp-looking rocks. They may be about the size of a bowling ball, but they're nowhere near as round and smooth.

As I got closer, I could see that the wreckage looked charred. Besides being black, which the underside of a car probably is anyway, the remains of the tires were hanging in shreds from the wheels. It took me a few minutes of careful maneuvering to make it down to the edge of the creek, and I noticed one of the younger men in the group had followed me down. I pulled my phone from my pocket to call 911 and discovered I had no signal, probably because I was a narrow valley between two steep slopes. I yelled up to the group at the top to call for assistance, and then I edged closer to the wreck. The young man moved closer as I looked into the creek to see whether I could wade safely to the car without stumbling on a slippery rock and falling on my keester.

"Can you make it?" he asked.

"Yeah, I think so. At least the water's pretty shallow right now. A couple of times they've had to open the valve after a heavy storm to lower the lake a bit, and then it becomes a real torrent."

I edged into the water, which was surprisingly chilly, but then I remembered that the outflow probably came from somewhere well below the surface of the lake where the water would be colder. Amazingly, I made it to the wreck without falling. I grabbed a piece of metal for support and realized my hand was now coated with greasy soot.

Because the car had landed on its roof, that was pretty much crushed. There was no glass in the windows, so I bent down nearly to the water to look inside. "Oh God!" I exclaimed.

"What's wrong?"

"There are bodies inside. It looks like two, and one of them's in the back seat in something that looks like it could have been a car seat." I didn't mention to the man that I'd already seen the two bodies lying alongside the trail earlier. There are some things you do not talk about to strangers.

"Are you sure they're dead?"

Was this guy serious? "Yeah, I'd say they are because they're pretty well toasted." Now it was his turn to turn green, but I didn't really care.

I stood up and looked over the bottom of the car, now the top. I noticed that the gas tank had a number of metal shards sticking up from a large hole, probably exploded. I hoped the two people inside had died quickly and with little or no pain.

I made my way back to the bank where the man had waited for me. "No point in trying to get them out. Maybe the cops can figure out what happened. It's probably better we don't touch anything because there's nothing we can do for them now except pray."

We waited about fifteen minutes until a patrol car, lights flashing and siren screaming, screeched to a halt on the road at the top of the steep slope. Two uniformed officers jumped out and started working their way down the hill, moving carefully to keep from toppling down. At least that side was grassy and not rocky like the face of the dam.

One of the officers, a woman, looked across the creek toward me after she reached the far bank. "Three-Zee, is that you?"

"Yeah, it's me. Hi, Liz." I'd met Liz Heyer last fall when she wound up investigating a series of incidents at our Haunted Woods event. She was a rookie then, and I wondered whether she was now considered a seasoned veteran. Anyway, I certainly wouldn't have wanted to be stuck investigating this mess.

By now the other officer had reached the bottom of the hill. "Hi, Hank," I said. Hank Kinsey, an older curmudgeon, had been Liz's partner last fall. Apparently, he still was—her partner, that is. The curmudgeon evaluation would come later.

"Oh God!" he exclaimed. "Not you again." We never had become besties, and it looked like that wasn't about to happen now, either. Okay, now he had requalified as a curmudgeon.

"Yeah, me, but you can't pin this one on me."

"Sure I can. You drove the car off the road and then jumped out when it rolled down the hill. Then you went home to bed like nothing happened."

"Tell that to the two inside. One of them's still in the driver's seat."

"Oh, well, I'll think of something."

"I'm sure you will."

"It looks like a kid in the back seat," Liz said. She'd waded into the creek and was bent over, looking through the hole where once there had been a back window.

"Oh, just what I needed," Hank said. "I knew this day was going to end badly."

"Hey, the day's not over, so maybe things will improve." Some people might consider this bear baiting, but I sometimes like to live dangerously.

Hank glared at me and grunted something, probably obscene. Then he waded into the creek to join Liz.

I glanced at my phone. Damn! It was time to start back with the hikers or they'd miss lunch, and nobody wanted to do that.

"Do you mind if I leave? I must get the hikers back to the lodge."

"Go, please go," Hank said. "I'm sure Liz and I can handle this. It's not the first car crash we've had to investigate."

"No, I'm sure it isn't." I turned and started up the face of the dam, followed again by the hiker who'd joined me by the creek. Going up was harder on the breath but a lot easier on the balance.

** ** **

"Okay, troop," I addressed my hikers. "It's time to get back to the lodge, so you folks can chow down."

"Don't you think you should stick around here in case those cops want to ask you more questions?" said the man who'd followed me down to the wreck and then back up.

"Yeah, it probably would be a good idea, but I must get you folks back."

"It's okay. I can lead them back. We'll return the way we came, and I'm sure we won't get lost."

"Er, okay, Mr., er, you do have a name, don't you?"

"DJ Jasper. I go by my initials. My first name's Darwin and my parents never gave me a middle name, but I don't like Darwin, so I just go by DJ."

"Well, yeah, Three-Zee really is my initials in a way. I appreciate the offer as long as you make sure nobody jumps into the lake and drowns."

DJ laughed. "I promise I'll rescue whoever tries to do that."

"Don't you think you should stick around for questioning, too? I mean, you were down there at the wreck with me."

"Yeah, but I know even less about what goes on here than you do. They might ask about what happened last night, and I know no more about that than any other of these hikers."

"Well, I really don't, either, but I guess as a person of authority, I'm the one they'd want to interrogate." This being a person of authority was getting old fast.

I watched as DJ led the group back the way we'd come. I decided I could schedule another 'Round-the-Lake walk later in the week for those people who felt they'd missed the second half of the trek.

I walked to the top edge of the dam face to try to see what was happening below. Liz and Hank were still standing on the far bank of the creek while more people had arrived. I noticed several more vehicles parked on the road: another patrol car, an ambulance, and a wrecker. I'm sure nobody was thrilled about the task that lay before them.

I had just turned my back on that depressing scene to look out over the peaceful lake when a shimmer appeared between me and the water's edge. The shimmer became a young woman and little boy fading into view. The little boy appeared to be around three or four.

"Can you see us?" the woman asked. She was around five-seven with well-cut long, dark hair, and slender with a rather narrow face.

"Yeah, you and the boy. I assume he's your son." The boy certainly had her coloring.

The little boy grinned. "She's my mommy," he said proudly.

"Are you from the car wreck down in the creek?"

"I don't know," the woman replied looking very confused. "Are we? I'm not sure where we are or how we got here."

"I think you wrecked your car over on the road below here. You probably went off the road and rolled down the hill, ending up in the creek."

"And were killed in the wreck?"

"Yeah." I decided not to go into details about the condition of their bodies. There are some things it's better people and ghosts don't know.

My experience with ghosts, and I've had a fair amount, is that they usually don't know or remember the conditions relating to their deaths. That's probably a good thing, especially if that death was accompanied by terrible fear or pain. It's also hard to tell how far before or after the death the memories are clipped, which seems to vary by person.

"When did you realize you were, er, deceased?"

"I'm not quite sure. We were able to climb that rocky hill without gasping for breath, and I'm so out of shape I usually get out of breath just climbing a flight of stairs. Then there was that group of people who just walked away from here. We were standing right there with them, yet nobody seemed to see us. Then somehow I knew I could fade in and out, which is certainly something I've never been able to do before."

"That rocky hill is the face of our dam here at Mountain Woods Resort, and this is our lake. What's the last thing you remember?" I asked.

"I'm not sure. We were in my car stopped for a red light, and then some guy forced his way into the car. He was holding some sort of handgun and threatened to kill my son if I didn't take him somewhere and then leave him with the car."

"Take him where?"

"I don't know. I remember driving away with him sitting beside me in the front seat and telling me to turn, and that's all I remember. The next thing I know, we were climbing that hill, er, dam face. You aren't dead, are you?"

"No, or at least I wasn't before you just faded into view."

"So, how is it you can see us?"

"I don't have the foggiest idea. As far as I know, the only people here at Mountain Woods who can see and hear you are me and my best friend, Bambi. Oh, and Snickers can, too. He's my cat."

"I've always heard that cats have special powers."

"Yeah, and Snickers has them in spades."

"So, what do we do now?"

"I'm not sure. You probably won't be able to move on until you find out how you died and, in your case, who that guy was who was hijacking your car."

"Move on?"

"Don't ask. I have no idea where to. All I know is that most ghosts move on after they learn the details of their deaths."

"Did you say we're at the Mountain Woods Resort?"

"Yeah, why?"

"That's at least ten miles from where we were hijacked."

"Hm. Can you give me a description of the man who kidnapped you?"

"It was pretty dark, but I'd say he was maybe in his late thirties or early forties with light-colored hair and clean-shaven. I didn't notice any sort of tattoos or other distinguishing marks, but I was mostly trying to drive and not go off the road. I was terrified he'd shoot my boy—he kept threatening to. Was Johnny shot? I don't see any wounds."

"You probably won't. I've met quite a few ghosts over the years, and none of them has shown evidence of how they were killed. In any case, it really doesn't matter."

"Oh."

I turned my back on the pair and walked over to look down at the wreck. Activity was continuing. I noticed a couple of men lugging a body bag up the hill, and the wrecker crew was hauling the end of a long winch cable down to attach to what remained of the car.

The woman and boy had walked to my side. "Was that my car?"

"Yeah, I'd say so."

"Probably not going to bring much at auction." I turned to look at the woman. She'd just been through what had to have been a terrible death, both she and her little boy, yet she was able to joke about it. I guess I'll never understand ghosts.

Home with New Friends

I noticed that Liz and Hank were getting into their patrol car, so I decided they probably didn't want to grill me about what I knew, which was next to nothing anyway. Besides, if they wanted me, they knew where to find me.

I turned to the ghosts, mother and son. "Let's hike back to the lodge. You can hang out in my cottage until I get back at dinnertime."

"What about food for us? I can't imagine how I'd pay for it."

"You won't have to because you won't get hungry or have to eat, or drink for that matter. Actually, you can't die of thirst or starvation or drowning or anything else because you're already dead. Unfortunately, there are drawbacks, too." I set out walking along the trail with the woman at my side and little Johnny trailing behind us.

"What kind of drawbacks?"

"Well, you're stuck wearing what you have on now, at least until you move on. After that, who knows? Also, eating and drinking, while possible, are extremely difficult because you can't pick anything up. You can sit on stuff and walk on stuff—solid surfaces seem to work vertically— but horizontally you can walk right through stuff including walls, buildings, furniture, people, whatever."

"So, when we come to a door, we don't have to open it but can walk right through it."

"Right, but then you wouldn't be able to turn the doorknob anyway. Your hand would go right through that, too." I turned my head to look at the woman. "By the way, you mentioned that your son is named Johnny, but you never told me your name."

"Lauren Capobianco. My little boy's first name is actually Giovanni—we're Sicilian through and through—but we all call him Johnny."

"What kind of car were you driving? It was too beat up for me to tell although I'm sure the cops were able to figure it out."

"A new BMW or Beemer. Only about five thousand miles on it. It was a gift from my father."

"Nice gift. And your husband? I guess he'll have to be notified."

"Yeah, well, I'm sure the cops will take care of that—my father, too."

"Mm. I'm sure they won't be happy about it."

"No, and believe me, if they identify that guy who carjacked me and he's still alive—well, I wouldn't want to be in his shoes."

By now we'd nearly reached the lodge, but I turned and headed down the lane that led past our cottage. I opened the door to enter, and Lauren and Johnny followed me inside.

"Okay, this is my cottage. Actually, it's where both Bambi and I hang our hats and other clothes when we aren't wearing them. Decent beds, too."

Snickers came out of the bedroom and stared at the newcomers curiously. "And this is Snickers who either can see you or likes to stare directly at the place where you are."

"Pussycat," Johnny exclaimed gleefully, running toward the cat. Surprisingly, Snickers didn't pull back or run away, but let the boy pet him. I suspected neither of them actually felt anything except that Snickers probably was experiencing that chill that comes with making contact with a ghost. However, he didn't seem to mind. As far as I knew, he'd never been around small children before.

I pulled my phone from my pocket and glanced at the time. "Whoops. I must get back to my office for a meeting with my boss; actually, a couple of layers of bosses. Anyway, you probably should hang around in here—Johnny can play with Snickers, and you can sit and wait. I don't think you can take a nap or anything like that, but I'm never quite sure about all your limitations. Anyway, I'll send Pete here if I run into him."

"Pete?"

"Oh yeah, he's my big boss's stepson."

"And he can see me?"

"Pete's like you, a ghost."

"Why hasn't he moved on?"

"He's got the hots for Bambi, so he hangs around."

"Bambi?"

"My roommate. Don't ask."

"Is she dead, too?"

"No, not in the least. I don't try to explain it. I just go with the flow."

As I left the cottage I looked back at Lauren's face. She looked totally confused, and frankly, I couldn't blame her. Meanwhile, Johnny was happily playing some kind of game of tag with Snickers.

✷✷ ✷✷ ✷✷

I was walking through a staff hallway on my way to George's office when I passed Pete coming from the direction of the indoor pool. I figured he was probably in there checking out the girls in their bikinis. We cater to a rather broad spectrum, both young and old, so there are usually a couple of younger women, some quite shapely. You might wonder why Pete was checking out the bikinis when he also claims to be enamored of Bambi. Again, don't ask. Anyway, I told him briefly about Lauren and Johnny and dispatched him to the cottage. He might have been on his way to the kitchen to watch Bambi at work, but he'd just have to wait for that.

I reached George's office, said hello to his secretary, Marlene Finsbury, and entered the inner sanctum. George sat behind his desk. Cathy Schwartz, activities director and my immediate supervisor, occupied a chair in front of it next to a young woman I'd never seen before. I sat in the remaining chair.

"What the heck was that kerfuffle this morning?" George asked as soon as my butt hit the chair.

"Er, what kerfuffle? Oh, the wreck in the creek."

"Yeah, that kerfuffle. It'll be all over the papers again."

"George, how the heck can a wrecked car in the creek at the base of our dam be blamed on me or the resort. It came off a public road that anybody could have been traveling, and it just happened to land where it did. We didn't build the road, we don't own the property where the road is, and we have no ability to control who might be using the road. Heck, I'm not even sure we own the property where the car landed."

"Actually, we do for about ten feet beyond the creek, so it was on our land, but you *would* have to be the person who found the wreck."

"Well, technically, it was one of our guests who saw it first, but yeah, I was the one who stumbled down the face of the dam to investigate. Still, what if the people inside had still been alive? I could have been the one to save their lives."

"But they were already dead."

"Yes, they were already dead."

"Did you...?"

"I'll tell you about it later." Cathy and the young stranger both looked at me curiously, but I wasn't about to discuss ghost sightings with either one of them. George knows about my ability although I'm not sure how much he believes.

"Anyway," George went on, "keep me posted on what the police find out."

"Yeah, if they even stoop so low as to tell me. They don't like to share stuff with the likes of me. Liz Heyer is okay. She was the first one at the wreck. But her partner, Hank Kinsey, considers me to be somewhat lower than whale poop."

"Mm, yes, I've met Mr. Kinsey. He doesn't have the best bedside manner."

"So, now that we've gotten that out of the way for the moment, why am I here?"

"We want to discuss the riding stable."

"A good idea, of course. Do you have a date when we can start getting horses?"

"The builder is telling me about two weeks. I went over there this morning, and it looks like he'll be able to make it. Meanwhile, we must start buying appropriate animals and then caring for them once they arrive."

"Were you expecting me to do that? I have some small experience with horses—we always had at least one on our farm except now. However, Old Thunderbolt died last year and Mom and Aunt Gladys decided not to replace him. I'm really not a qualified wrangler. I think you'll need somebody dedicated to the job who can be responsible for the horses, know a lot about their care and feeding, maintain the tack for the riders, and even, maybe, schedule and lead trail rides. I can ride and lead some, but I'd probably have to neglect some of my other duties if that became a full-time job."

"Yes, we understand, which is why this young woman is sitting here."

"Oh." I looked at her—five-seven or thereabouts, slim, blond, pretty face, probably early twenties, would definitely be a hit with the young male guests.

Cathy looked at me and said, "We did some searching for candidates and this young woman popped up. I hope you don't mind we didn't get you involved in the interviewing, but you've been busy with your regular job."

"No, I don't mind at all." I looked at the new wrangler because from the way Cathy had worded that last statement, I was pretty sure she'd already been hired. "Er, can I ask you your name?"

"Of course," she said, the first words she'd spoken since I entered the office, so at least she didn't seem to be an annoying chatterbox. "I'm Elizabeth Borden, but my friends all call me Lizzie."

"And in case these two haven't already told you," I made a sweeping gesture that covered Cathy and George, "I'm Zelanie Zook, known to my friends as Three-Zee."

"That's an odd nickname."

"Believe me, if your name were Zelanie Zephora Zook, you'd welcome it." The girl winced when I mentioned my full name. At least she had taste. "By the way, Lizzie Borden sounds familiar somehow. Have we ever met?"

"Okay, let me make something clear. I am not from Attleboro, Massachusetts, nor from anywhere in Massachusetts for that matter. Also, I did not take an axe and give forty whacks to my mother, nor did I use one to give forty-one whacks to my father. Both my parents are very much alive, thank you very much."

"Sorry. I didn't mean to offend you although I had forgotten about the poem."

"That's okay. I'm kind of used to it."

"So, how did you get into the wrangling business?"

"My parents used to own a riding stable in Bucks County down near Philadelphia, and I worked for them as a wrangler since I was in my early teens. However, they sold out and retired a few months ago, and the new owners and I didn't agree on things, so I quit."

"Yeah, I can see where new people might want to make some changes that the former owners might not approve of." I turned in my seat so I could see all three people. "Have you identified any sources for horses?"

"There are quite a few listings on the internet," Cathy said, "and I've looked into a few. Also, there are some local places. However, I'm not really qualified to judge, so I'll leave that up to Lizzie to make the evaluations."

"Like a horse of a different color," I said, but nobody laughed, so I decided to cut out the wisecracks for the moment.

"Where will I be able to work?" Lizzie asked.

"Temporarily, you can share the small office that Three-Zee's been using," Cathy said. "That is, if Three-Zee doesn't mind." I shook my head to indicate I didn't mind at all. I rarely used the office anyway. "The new stable building will have an office and apartment for you as well as a tack room, places for hay and feed storage, rest rooms, and other necessities. We hired a professional designer to plan the building layout."

"Yes, that sounds good. I'm looking forward to working with all of you," Lizzie said. Those were all the right things for a new employee to say, but it might take a while to be sure she really meant it.

Grillings

The afternoon went smoothly. I ran a Bingo game at two. It never ceases to amaze me how many people go to an expensive resort, and then on a warm spring day when the outdoors is beckoning, the lake is full of fish, and the indoor pool is fully operational—in late April opening the outdoor pool wouldn't make sense except for polar bears and penguins—they opt to stay indoors and play Bingo or some other game. We make money on it, so we do it.

I finished and got everything put away by four, and then I headed to the cottage to see my new guests. I opened the door to find Lauren sitting on the sofa, Johnny on the floor with Snickers curled up next to him, and Pete on the easy chair. "So, how did it go," I asked.

"How did what go?" Pete answered.

"Okay, I suppose that wasn't clear. How did your ghost training session go?"

"Oh, that. Well, ghosts really don't need a lot of training. We mostly learn by doing or not doing if we can't do."

"No, I guess there wouldn't be any schools or colleges for ghosts to become proficient. Maybe after they move on, but none of us knows anything about that."

"Correct. Anyway, I've been trying to get Lauren here to remember what happened closer to the time of the accident."

I looked at Lauren. "And have you remembered more?"

"Maybe a little bit. Like I told you earlier, he pulled a gun on me and then got into my car while I was stopped at a red light on the highway. No other cars were around at the time. I went straight through the light—it was green by then—and then drove another few miles and passed maybe a couple more lights—I'm not sure about that—until he told me to turn right onto a narrower paved road. I remember that road as being quite curvy and hilly, but that's where everything goes blank."

"Mm, well, the road past the dam, the one where you went off the road and down the hill, fits the description of being hilly and curvy. It's not too heavily traveled, so if you went off the road in the middle of the night, probably nobody would have come along for a while. Otherwise, they might have seen the fire and reported it. How come you were out driving so late?"

"I was lost. I've never been in this area before—I was passing through on the interstate—and I noticed my gas was getting low, so I got off and started looking for a gas station. However, I remember it was around midnight, and nothing was open."

"Yeah, they roll up the streets pretty early around here. There are a couple of minimarts that sell gas and are open all night, but you have to know where to find them."

"I finally did find one and was planning to turn into its lot after the light changed, but that's when the guy pulled the gun on me."

"Bad timing. Where are you from?"

"Philly. My dad's a, well, I'd better not say."

"Oh?"

"Okay, he's a big wheel in the Sicilian brotherhood."

"Sort of like a godfather?"

"Definitely like a godfather. My husband's one of his lieutenants."

"Ah. I suppose they won't be happy when they find out."

"My father will probably blame my husband because I was on my way to Pottsville to join him. My husband has some business contacts there, and after he met with them, we were going to stay overnight there and then drive to Pittsburgh this morning."

"Weren't you running a bit late? Surely your husband wouldn't be having a business meeting at midnight."

"Yes, I was running late. I didn't get on the road until after ten, and I ran into a traffic jam caused by an accident down around Norristown somewhere. I've never been very good with directions, so I think I made a couple of wrong turns trying to get around the accident and wound up here."

"Didn't your car have a GPS?" I asked.

"Yeah, but I liked the one on my phone better, so I was using that. At some point my phone stopped talking to me. I think I forgot to charge it yesterday, and I didn't have it plugged into a charger cable in the car. I should have activated the car's GPS or dug out the charger cable for my phone, but I thought I could find a town as big as Pottsville without the help."

"You wouldn't have easily. You were going pretty much in the wrong direction. So, what happens now?"

"Well, like I said, I'm sure my father will blame my husband because I was going to join him. I'm an only child, or I guess I should say, 'I *was* an only child,' and Johnny's the only grandchild."

"You make it sound like your father can get nasty," I said. So far, her description of the man didn't seem to make him a person I wanted to meet.

"Oh yeah. My husband will be lucky to come out of this in one piece."

I'd recently had to deal with some vindictive thugs, although fortunately I wasn't the one on their radar, so I could understand how dicey things could get for those who were.

"Have you remembered anything else about your kidnapper?"

"No. Like I said, he was in his late thirties or early forties with light-colored hair and clean-shaven, and I didn't notice any tattoos or scars or other marks. It was too dark to make out much else, and I was really nervous about my driving, so I tried to pay attention to the road."

"Do you think he could have had something to do with your father's business, like maybe a rival gang or something?"

"If I had been in the Philly area or even in Pottsville where I was headed, maybe. However, I doubt anybody I know would have had any idea where I was. Remember, I was lost."

"Yes, very lost."

I was just about to leave again and head up to the lodge where I could grab something to eat at the employee dining room when somebody knocked on the cottage door. I opened it to find Liz Heyer standing on the doorstep.

"Hey, Liz. What's new?"

"I came here to find that out from you."

I led Liz to the easy chair. Pete moved out of it to keep Liz from feeling the chill when she occupied the same space. I plopped down on the sofa again next to Lauren.

"What's with your cat?" Liz asked.

"What do you mean?"

"Well, he's acting almost like somebody's petting him, but he's all alone there on the floor."

Johnny *was* petting him, but Liz can't see or hear ghosts. "Oh, you know how crazy cats can be. I don't try to figure him out."

"Yeah, you're probably right. Anyway, I wanted to ask you a few more questions about the accident."

"Sure, but like I said earlier, I don't know much more about it than you do, maybe less now that your minions have had a chance to go over the wreckage."

"Okay, they were able to identify the car from the license plate. The lettering was all burned off, but that's one of the reasons the metal is embossed so you still can read them. If that wouldn't have worked, the vehicle's VIN number is engraved on a number of parts, so we nearly always can make a quick ID."

"And...?"

"The car was registered to a Giovanni Capobianco from Philadelphia." Out of the corner of my eye, I could see Lauren nodding, but I tried not to look at her because Liz would have wondered why I was looking to my side at the empty, to her, sofa. "We're guessing the victims were his wife and son, but we won't be sure until we can check for a DNA match. The Philly police are getting some DNA samples for us to compare."

"Yeah."

"What do you mean, yeah? Do you know something we don't?"

Oops. Three-Zee, Liz doesn't know about you and ghosts. Try to keep your foot out of your mouth. "No, of course not. I was just agreeing with you about the procedure."

Liz gave me a curious look, but then she went on. "I really shouldn't be telling you this, but we're pretty sure Lauren's husband—Lauren is the name of the victim if she's who we think she is—has ties to the Philadelphia mob."

"Do you think it was some kind of hit?"

"We don't know, but it's certainly possible. At the moment we have no idea why she would have been driving on that road at night. We're assuming it was during the night because nobody reported seeing the wreck earlier. Unfortunately, the bodies were so badly burned that it's going to be nearly impossible to figure out the time of death. In the old days you could look at a smashed watch or car clock and say with some certainty that the accident happened at the time it stopped, but with digital technology and chips, all that got fried in the fire, so there's no information about time." During this rather macabre description I saw Lauren wince. I had discovered that even ghosts don't like to think about the gory details. Johnny, at least, was too young for any of this to bother him.

"Wasn't the woman, Lauren, wearing a watch?"

"Yeah, but one of those watches that connects to a phone, so it's all chips and displays, too, and it was equally fried."

"Have you notified next of kin yet?"

"I think the Philly cops are doing that because they'll need access to her house to gather DNA evidence. However, we have to be careful, because if it's not her, we'll really open a can of worms."

"Yeah, I can see where that would be a problem, especially if her husband's in the mob."

"So, what can you tell me?" Liz asked.

"Tell you? Oh, about the accident. Well, nothing more than I told you this afternoon. One of the women on the hike I was leading was looking down the face of the dam and saw the wreckage in the outflow creek. I knew it hadn't been there yesterday morning because I'd led another hike that way, and I remember looking down at the creek to see how fast it was running."

"And you clambered down that rocky slope to investigate."

"Yes, of course. It was possible somebody was in the wreck and was alive. I didn't realize the car had burned until I was halfway down the hill, but even then I thought it was worth checking out."

"That guy who was with you. Is he one of the customers here?"

"Guests. Yeah, his name is DJ Jasper. He said you can look him up here if you need to talk to him."

"DJ?"

"He said his name's Darwin with no middle initial, hence DJ."

"You don't happen to know his room number, do you?"

"No, but the front desk can give you everything you need. I have a list in my office of everybody who signed up for the hike, but the front desk doesn't need that because there's no extra charge for the hikes. I can get it for you if you want it."

"Yeah, it would be helpful."

"Okay. I was just about to head up there to get something to eat, so I'll dig it out." I got up, pulled on a sweatshirt—the nights still get chilly in late April—and led the way out the door.

"Are your meals included?" Liz asked as we started up the lane toward the main lodge.

"Such as they are, yes."

An Unexpected Guest

"Damn!" I was passing George in the hall as he was just tucking his phone into his pocket. The exclamation was rather unexpected, to say the least.

"Is everything okay?" I asked.

George spun around to focus on me. "No, it's not!" he snapped.

"Oh, sorry." I wasn't sure why I was apologizing, but at that moment George looked like a rabid wolf, definitely someone to be avoided at all costs. Then his features relaxed, and he exhaled.

"No, Three-Zee, I'm sorry. It's not your fault."

"May I ask what's not my fault?"

"Marvin Pendergast."

"Well, I'm glad he's not my fault, but who the heck is Marvin Pendergast?"

"A member of the board."

"The board of Mountain Springs?"

"Yeah, that board. Son of a b… Sorry."

"Is he also a part owner?"

"Everybody on the board is a part owner, which is why they're on the board. Unfortunately, Marvin owns the largest percentage."

"Controlling?" I don't know much about boards of directors, but I was pretty sure a person needed to own more than fifty percent in order to have a controlling interest. Anyway, the word sounded to me like I knew what I was talking about.

"No, nobody has control, but Pendergast has a couple of pals who, with his percentage, do add up to more than half."

"Oh. So, why are you so pissed off about Marvin Pendergast?"

"He's a scumbag."

"Yeah, I kind of get that, but is he up to something you don't approve of?"

"Not exactly."

"So, what's the problem?"

"He's coming here."

"Here?"

"Yeah, here, as a guest for a couple of weeks."

"Well, I guess he has that right."

"Yeah, he does, but Marvin will expect royal treatment and won't pay a dime. Don't look for compliments or tips."

"Like 'Don't take any wooden nickels'?"

"Not even that."

"When's he coming?"

"Tomorrow. He'll want the royal suite."

"Royal suite? I didn't know we had a royal suite."

"We don't, but that one on the top floor that overlooks the lake is the closest we have. It's always the first choice for a bridal suite. We just modify the decorations."

"Is anybody occupying it now? I'm sure he wouldn't throw out a paying guest just to have the best room."

"I don't think anybody's in there now, but I'll have to check with reservations. They might have somebody booked."

"Yeah, I would do that. If they have somebody already there or booked, I'm sure Mr. Pendergast would accept a different room."

"You don't know Marvin."

"No, but I get the feeling I'm going to."

** ** **

I didn't have a hike or anything else scheduled for this morning, so I decided to take a walk to the construction site for the new stable building. Before I left, I stuck my head into my office to see whether Lizzie was in there, but she wasn't.

The riding stable will be in back of the lodge, on the far side from the lake and outdoor pool, and behind the employee dormitory building and employee parking lot. Currently, the outside is more or less finished, but a number of workers are still working on the inside. I wasn't surprised to find Lizzie standing just outside one of the big barn doors staring in. It was the first I'd seen her standing up, and she was tall and slender; okay, not really tall, I'd say around five-seven, but I'm only five-two, so to me she was tall.

"So, how's it going?" I asked.

"It's going, I guess," Lizzie replied.

"Do you like what you see so far?"

"Yeah, it'll be good. My folks' place wasn't nearly this fancy."

"No, but then their guests might not have been as wealthy or fussy."

"Oh, some of them were. There's a lot of money in Bucks County, old money, and we were close enough to the city. However, we boarded horses for some of the ordinary folks, too, and we tried not to make anybody feel out of place."

"That's a good way to handle things. Not everybody was born with a silver spoon. Although my parents weren't poor, I'm pretty sure my spoon was plastic."

"Too much plastic in this world."

"Yeah, I agree there. Is your new office finished?"

"Almost. I was in there a few minutes ago, but it was just painted this morning, and the smell was driving me crazy."

"How about office furniture?"

"It's supposed to show up later this week. Then I guess I can start moving in."

"I'm not sure whether we have any suitable riding trails. I know we have a couple of good hiking trails, especially the one that goes around the lake, and there's the forest road, which isn't paved. Also, I know horses do best when they're not on paved surfaces. We have a lot of Amish farms down where I lived, and their horses sometimes suffer a bit from trotting on the roads."

"You're right. I must get to know the property to see what's here. I'm not sure about the lakeshore because I don't want a horse to get spooked and throw its rider into the water. Is the trail safe enough for horses—no rocky areas and stuff like that?"

"There are some rocky and narrow parts, and the top of the dam and the new bridge across the spillway might not be appropriate. I think the bridge is strong enough, but crossing that spillway might be a bit scary for an animal. Heck, sometimes it's scary for me."

"Yeah, at least until the horses become used to it. Maybe there are some other trails."

"Well, I know there are a couple to the right of the forest road, but I seldom venture into that area. The trails to the left go down to Abner's old trailer where we had the Haunted Woods last fall, and from there you can ride about a half mile out to the paved state highway on the access lane, which isn't paved. Below the pond you can get on the lakeshore trail, and that'll take you to the spillway bridge."

"Abner? Is he a resort employee?"

"Hardly. He used to own a wedge of property that kept us from building a trail to circumnavigate the lake. There's a pond on the main feeder stream to the lake, accessible by boat from the lake itself. Abner was a real old curmudgeon who had a little something going on on the side. He used to take potshots at our guests if they ventured into the creek. Bambi got some shotgun pellets in her thigh one night. Let's just say we probably were boating in the dark where we shouldn't have been. Anyway, Abner is now getting free room and board from the Commonwealth of Pennsylvania in one of its luxurious accommodations, and the resort now owns his property. Oh, and the old trailer he used to live in has been hauled away, and we're going to bring in a new double-wide to take its place and function as an office for future activities in the area."

"Mm, well, that sounds like a good ride. I guess I should plan to check out those other trails, too, the ones you said you don't know much about."

"Yeah, I don't know why I never got around to hiking up there. I just never think of it on my days off to scout those out."

"By the way, who's Bambi?"

"Oh, she's my cottage mate. We've been best friends since we were kids; she lived on a nearby farm. She works in the kitchen as a line cook and trainee chef, and she also helps out on the registration desk when they get busy, especially on Sunday mornings when we have our biggest turnover. By the way, have you moved into the employee housing yet?"

"Yeah, I'm sharing a room with a girl named Shirley. I think she's a server in the dining room and lounge. I know she came in late last night."

"Mm. We'll probably have to realign your room so you're sharing with somebody on a similar schedule to yours. Otherwise, neither one of you will get much sleep."

"They told me this is temporary until that new apartment is finished for me here in the stable building."

"Just think, your own stall, and all the oats and hay you can eat."

Lizzie laughed. "Yeah, but it'll be *my* stall, and the horses won't be coming in at all hours of the night."

"If they do, they'll be genuine party animals."

** ** **

Bambi and I met in the employee dining room at six because Bambi had worked the breakfast and lunch shift. We had never really become close to any of the other employees, partially because we didn't live in the same building, and, well, I'm not sure why not exactly. Anyway, Lizzie seemed like she might be a good fit for our personalities, and she'd be somewhat of a loner herself, living in the stable building as she would be, so I planned to introduce her to Bambi as soon as possible. Also, like me, Bambi had some limited riding experience because her folks had kept a pony for her when she was a child and a full-size horse later. There are definite advantages to living on a farm.

"Who's this Marvin Pendergast they were talking about in the kitchen?" Bambi asked after we'd carried our trays to a table.

"I guess he's one of the owners. George doesn't like him. Says he's a pain in the butt."

"Yeah, that was the consensus of the old-timers in the kitchen, too. He shows up here every year or so for a week or two and complains about everything."

"Funny, I don't remember him from last year."

"He decided to show up and try to run things while we were all at Cape Cod last spring. I guess George was really happy he didn't have to be here and put up with him, but Marvelous Marvin—that's what they call him in the kitchen—was on everybody's case while he was here. Anyway, he sounds like a person I don't want to meet."

"No, from what I hear, I don't think I want to, either."

"Well, he's getting the bridal suite tomorrow night," Bambi said. "Fortunately, nobody is in it this week or next. Last year he was furious he had to take a lesser suite because a bride and groom were already occupying it."

"From what I hear about him, I'm surprised he didn't kick them out and make them take one of the cheap rooms," I said. "After all, they were only paying guests."

"Yeah, I guess nobody would have been surprised."

Unwelcome Guests

I'm sure it's an issue at every resort, hotel, motel, inn, and bed and breakfast in the world. There are guests you simply don't want, can't tolerate, and wish would go somewhere else, in some cases to the bottom of a high cliff from which they'd just fallen. Not everybody is a nice, caring person, except maybe in caring about themselves.

We were destined to get one of those guests on Thursday afternoon, and from what I'd heard about him, I wasn't looking forward to it. Was he arrogant because he was rich and part owner of the resort, or was he rich and part owner of the resort because he was arrogant? That's a question that's hard to answer, so I won't try.

I led a 'Round-the-Lake hike on Thursday morning, more or less a reprise of the aborted Tuesday morning hike, and many of the same guests took this one, I think to see what lay on the far side of the spillway bridge. At least this time when I looked down the dam face from the top, no overturned vehicles cluttered the outflow creek. Only the usual collection of rocks dotted the flowing water.

I was rather surprised that DJ hadn't joined us on this hike, especially as he had seemed quite enthusiastic about the last one. However, when I thought about it, I hadn't seen him around since then although I suppose I could have missed him. Many of our guests I never saw unless they happened to attend one of the activities I hosted.

Because her plate of duties wasn't yet very full, Lizzie joined us, partially to get the lay of the land, and partially to see whether the trail would be suitable for trail rides. She decided for the moment it would be too risky, especially with the top of the dam having steep drop-offs on each side and the spillway bridge never really being designed for horses. It was strong enough to bear their weight, but its railings were designed for people on foot and not mounted on horseback several feet in the air.

It still seemed a bit strange to see the bare spot where Abner's rusty old trailer had stood for who knows how many years. It wasn't much, but it had served him for a long time as his home, and it was a warm place to use as my onsite office during last fall's Haunted Woods event. As I'd told Lizzie, a new double-wide trailer, configured as an office and small lunchroom with restrooms, was ordered for the site, but it hadn't yet arrived. The lunchroom would have a serving window behind which was a limited kitchen for serving snacks, et cetera, during events, eliminating the need for an outdoor kiosk like the one we'd used last fall.

"Do you think we could at least use the trails from the pond up to here?" I asked after we'd made our way to the forest road.

"Yes, those will be fine. Also, this road will be excellent, at least as far as I can see. You said there are some trails on the other side?"

"A couple between here and the main road, which is at the end of this one. This road is unpaved all the way, but the state highway is paved. Also, there's a gate at the end of this road, which we only unlock when we need access. We did that last fall for the hay wagon that transported guests to the ghouls because it had to travel the state highway for a short distance. You can go around the gate if you're on foot, and I suspect a horse could navigate that, too."

"I noticed some construction materials down there at the end of the pond just below where you said the trailer used to be."

"Yeah, there was a dock, but it was so rickety it collapsed under the weight of one of the high school kids who was working as a zombie. He almost became one, but fortunately, he wasn't injured. Just cold and wet. Anyway, they're going to rebuild it so guests can row their boats, canoes, and kayaks right up to it. By then we hope to have the trailer in place, too, and we're thinking of operating a snack bar inside it at least part of the time. A lot depends on whether we can make any money at it."

"Mm, the eternal issue. Can we make any money at it?"

"I suppose, but this place doesn't pay our salaries and house and feed us without money."

"No, you're right. Humans don't function well when required to live like the wild animals."

"I, for one, wouldn't like to run around naked and subsist on roots, berries, and any slow mice I could catch."

Lizzie laughed. "Neither would I, and we certainly couldn't exist on a diet of grass like the wild horses."

I grinned and then bent over, tore off a tall blade of grass, and began sucking on it like a stereotypical hayseed farmer. "Tastes kind of poor," I noted.

** ** **

After we returned to the lodge, Lizzie and I made our way to the employee dining room to get some lunch. Bambi was on her break, so she joined us, and I introduced her to Lizzie.

"I was talking to Sandy in reception. She came back to the kitchen to grab a cup of coffee," Bambi said.

"And…"

"Marvelous Marvin's private secretary called and said he'd be here at around three. Housekeeping has been up in his suite removing the bridal suite décor and making it more masculine."

"Yeah, they do stuff like that all the time depending on the guests. No big deal."

"No, it isn't, but the other thing she told me is a big deal."

"Oh?"

"The godfather is coming."

"The who?"

"Okay, I don't know whether he's actually a godfather, but his name is Guido Corsana, and supposedly he's some bigwig in the Philadelphia mob."

"Do you think he's related to…" Oops, Three-Zee, Lizzie doesn't know you been speaking with the daughter of a Philadelphia mob boss or at least the ghost of the daughter of a Philadelphia mob boss.

Lizzie gave me a curious look. "Why did you suddenly stop talking?"

"Oh, it's nothing. It's just that we know a woman with ties like that."

"Yeah, we only know Lauren's married name, not her maiden one," Bambi explained.

"So, why do you say the godfather is coming?" I asked.

"I guess this guy has requested our best suite for himself plus rooms on each side for some of his associates."

"Well, the only way we could do that is to give him the bridal suite. There are six suites on the fifth floor, and the bridal suite is the nicest."

"That's the problem. He wants to show up tomorrow, and Marvelous Marvin is already booked for the bridal suite starting this afternoon. Also, that one's on the end, so there isn't one on each side. I guess that would be okay because if he's paranoid, nobody could get at him from that side except maybe Spiderman. The one on the other side is open, but if we give him those two suites, Marvelous Marvin would have to settle for a regular room on a lower floor because all the other suites on that floor are booked."

"Which would not go over well."

"No, I'm sure it would not."

"Bam, would you want to own a resort and deal with all these headaches?"

"Never in a million years."

** ** **

On my way back to the office Lizzie and I were currently sharing, I sent her on and ducked into George's office. Marlene was out, probably at her own lunch, so I barged in.

"What do *you* want?" he grumped. "Don't tell me you found another body in the creek. No, this one probably was in the woods or maybe in the lake."

"No, nothing like that. I just stopped in to ask about Mr. Corsana."

"I suppose that's all over the place by now."

"Did you think something like that would remain a secret? I mean, it's not every day we get a real godfather to stay here."

"Three-Zee, we don't know that. In fact, the only way I even suspect it is because one of our staff is from Philadelphia and started spreading the word about his reputation. The thing that kind of surprises me is that it's such a last-minute thing. Usually, when mobsters take vacations, they send their heavies out a couple of weeks in advance to start making sure the place meets their security standards."

"Which are very high."

"Extremely so. Why would he be coming here now?"

"His daughter."

"Huh?"

"I think the woman and little boy who died in the creek are his daughter and grandson."

"How would you know that? Did Officer Liz spill the beans?" He paused for a moment. "Oh, that's right. You've probably met their ghosts."

"Yes, I have. In fact, they were sitting in my living room with Pete this morning when I left for breakfast and little Johnny was playing with Snickers."

"Pete being my stepson."

"Yeah, that Pete."

"Mm. I guess I'll never figure it out. I want to believe you, I really do, but it's tough."

"I understand. If I wasn't me, I'd think I was crazy, too."

"Do you know, that statement makes no sense whatsoever. Anyway, are you sure she was this mobster's daughter?"

"No, I never asked her what her maiden name was, but she did say she was from Philly and her father is more-or-less a godfather. Her married name is Capobianco, and her husband is, I think, a hit man for her father. Too much coincidence there, don't you think?"

"I've reached the point where I don't know what I think. This does put me on the horns of a dilemma, though."

"Do dilemmas have horns?"

"Big pointy ones, like longhorn bulls. You know, of course, about Mr. Pendergast."

"Marvelous Marvin, yeah, you told me."

"Where the heck did you come up with that nickname? Okay, I guess it fits, but is there a word beginning with M that maybe signifies nasty, obnoxious, and a total SOB."

"Not that I can think of at the moment, but I'll let you know if one comes to mind."

"Please do that. Okay, Marvelous Marvin has requested, no, let's say demanded, the bridal suite. Unfortunately, so has Mr. Corsana, and Mr. Corsana has also requested the rooms next door to said suite. Well, there's no room on the one side because it's at the end of the hall, but I suspect that will partially satisfy his security instincts. There is an empty suite on the other side—it's still a slow season—God help us if this happens in June—but that's the only other empty room on that floor. Marvin might have to move to a room on a lower floor—there are several available—but he'll be very unhappy about it. Oh well, at least Mr. Corsana didn't demand the entire floor with locked access."

"Have one of Papa Guido's goons threaten Marvin with a gun. That should make him reconsider which room he wants."

"Three-Zee, I like your style of thinking. I'm glad I proposed to your mother. I may have lost a stepson, but I'll be gaining a smart stepdaughter."

"And you haven't actually lost your stepson. Heck, you might even be getting Bambi as your step-daughter-in-law."

"I'm going to pretend I didn't hear that."

"Probably a wise decision on your part, Daddy." I got up to leave. "Hey, how about Pain-in-the-ass Pendergast?"

"I like it. It even almost rhymes."

The First Pain

Mr. Pendergast showed up at around four p.m., only an hour later than he said he'd arrive. However, I guess when you're an important person, other peoples' schedules don't really matter. I wasn't busy, so I was hanging out in the lobby to see whether there'd be some kind of nuclear explosion when he was told about his room assignment. Bambi would have been there, too, but she was busy in the kitchen and couldn't get away. I did notice Pete over in the corner, so I suspected he was watching to report to his little deer about what happened.

A shiny black Jaguar SUV pulled up under the front canopy, and a small man, gray-haired and balding, with a pinched face and demeanor to match, got out. The man strutted into the lobby as if he owned the place, which, come to think of it, he did, or at least partially.

"I'm Marvin Pendergast," he announced loudly as soon as he reached the front desk.

"Yes sir, we've been expecting you," replied Sandy Wilburn, who was the on-duty receptionist.

"I'm booked into Room 506."

"I'm sorry, sir, but that room isn't available, so we've put you in 412."

"What do you mean, 412? I specifically requested your best suite."

"Yes sir, but another guest has reserved it and the adjacent suite. All the other suites on the fifth floor are already occupied."

"Well, kick the SOB out of 506."

"I'm afraid, sir, that that won't be possible."

"Where's George? I demand to see George."

"I've notified Mr. Wylie that you're here. He should be with us momentarily."

I was impressed with Sandy's unfazed attitude. It's true that hotel desk receptionists become rather calloused from dealing with difficult people, but this guy had the power to fire her on the spot.

I saw George emerge from the staff doorway beside the desk. Marvelous Marvin, or maybe Pain-in-the-ass Pendergast, spun around and snapped very loudly, "Wylie, get your butt over here." I've been told many times that it's totally improper to vent one's spleen on a subordinate in a public place, but this rear-end of a donkey apparently had never received that message. Also, I wondered whether George was really a subordinate. Yes, he didn't own quite as big a percentage of the property as did Pendergast, but he owned the second-largest chunk.

"Hello to you, too, Marv," George replied. I casually wandered closer to make sure I didn't miss anything.

"Why can't I have 506?"

"Because it's been reserved by somebody else."

"And 505?"

"Same problem."

"I had already reserved 506."

"Yes, yesterday, but somebody else has requested it. Since you're an employee of sorts or at least wouldn't be paying for the room, you must yield to paying guests."

"I'll have your head."

"I don't think you can do that, at least not without cooperation from several other owners. Anyway, I think we should continue this conversation in my office. I'm not sure it's appropriate for other guests to hear us airing our dirty linen." He turned and opened the door into the staff hallway, motioning Pendergast to precede him through it.

I turned to find Pete standing at my shoulder. "Pete," I whispered, "follow them and report back."

Pete grinned, saluted, and walked through the closed door.

I grinned at Sandy, flashed her the okay symbol with my fingers and thumb, and headed back to my own office. I dearly would have loved to be a fly on the wall of George's, but I figured I'd soon get a report from my own fly on the wall. I only hoped Marvin couldn't see ghosts.

** ** **

I was sitting behind my small desk—Lizzie was somewhere else, probably over at the stable—when Pete reappeared by walking through a wall.

"Why don't you use the door like everybody else?"

"The wall's a bit closer."

"At least you just proved that ghosts can be lazy. Okay, so what happened in there? I didn't hear any actual explosions although I guess George's office is far enough away that the sound would be rather muffled."

"Needless to say, Marvelous Marvin vented his spleen. However, Dad stood his ground, and Marvin wound up taking Room 412, but you could tell he was not happy about it."

"I'm not really familiar with the rooms. I've been in 506 because I was checking out a special setup for a bridal party, but I've never been in 412. Is it decent?"

"All the rooms here are at least decent, actually quite luxurious. Otherwise, we couldn't get away with charging what we do. 412 is one of the king-bed mini-suites, which means it has a half-partition between the bed area and a small sitting area. Normally I think that goes for around four hundred bucks a night for one person, plus an additional hundred for each additional guest."

"And 506? I never did hear the rate."

"Around a thou for a couple; two hundred for each additional person. Also, quite a lot extra for special décor."

"Wow! Not exactly a no tell motel."

"No, although I don't think we tell, either, judging from some of the couples I see here, and an occasional threesome or foursome."

"Yeah, that would be interesting, but I'm an innocent young lady who doesn't know about stuff like that."

I was intrigued that a ghost could actually choke. "You've got to be kidding," Pete said after he'd stopped coughing.

I chose not to reply. Anyway, Pete took off so he could relay everything to Bambi, which he could do by standing next to her in the kitchen while she did whatever. Her toughest job then would be to maintain a straight face as if she weren't listening to the latest gossip being spoken into her ear by her favorite ghost, rather like listening to Bluetooth earbuds.

** ** **

After a gourmet dinner in the employee dining room—hey, the mac and cheese was actually quite tasty—I wandered back to the cottage where I found Lauren sitting on the sofa telling a story to little Johnny. Unfortunately, it's not possible for a ghost to actually pick up a book or turn its pages, so they'd need any reading materials to be spread out in front of them. They have a similar problem with TV, although if it's already on and set to the correct channel, they can watch. Snickers was lying on my bed snoozing, something cats do exceptionally well, so I guess either he or Johnny had tired of their playdate.

I said hello to my guests and went into my room to change into shorts and tee shirt from my usual workday attire of business casual, something I can alter when I'm actually leading a hike. When I returned to the living room Pete had arrived and Bambi came in a couple of minutes later.

"What did you think of Marvelous Marvin?" Bambi asked. "Pete tells me he was very unhappy."

"A rich guy's lot is not a happy one," Pete added.

"Actually, I think that's 'a policeman's lot is not a happy one' and it's from *The Pirates of Penzance*," I said.

"Yeah, whatever."

"Marvin was really ticked off that he didn't get the room he wanted," I said. I would have used stronger language than "ticked off", but there was a child in the room with us, even though the child in question was a ghost.

I turned to Lauren. "You said your father was kind of a big wheel in the Philadelphia mob, didn't you?"

"Well, yes, I did say that."

"His name wouldn't happen to be Guido Corsana, would it?"

"Yes. How did you know?"

"He's coming here."

"Here? When?"

"I think tomorrow. He's ordered our best suite plus an adjacent one for his associates."

"Ah, associates. I think you mean his enforcers."

"Whatever he wants to call his security staff is okay by me. Anyway, he bumped one of our owners from that suite."

"Is that a problem?"

"Not in the least. That owner, part owner really, is the Marvin we were talking about. He's rather obnoxious, to say the least, so it was interesting to see him taken down a peg or two."

"Do you think my father will be able to see me?"

"I doubt it although I really don't know for sure. However, you'll be able to see him and even hang around him. Little Johnny can see his grandfather, too, but grandpa probably won't be able to see him. Do you think your husband will come along?"

"I don't know. He was on that special assignment, but usually those don't last too long, so he might."

"Lauren, how much do you know about your father's and your husband's business dealings?"

"I know I've had a comfortable life—okay, did have a comfortable life—so I learned not to ask too many questions."

"Mm. Makes sense to me. The less you know, the better off you are."

The Second Pain

Lizzie showed up in the office in the morning with good news, at least for her. The portion of the stables where the horses would be housed was finished. Only her office and living space needed some additional work, but there was nothing that would prevent her from bringing in her first equine tenants.

Also, she had friends who had friends, and two horses were going to arrive by trailer tomorrow. The initial plan was for at least a half-dozen, but the others would require additional vetting before they were purchased and delivered. I agreed, weather permitting, I'd go riding with her Sunday afternoon to check out the trails.

Today, however, was rather gloomy with heavy clouds threatening rain at any moment. At least the forecasters had called this one right. I had canceled the scheduled morning hike—nobody wants to be walking through a dripping forest or, even worse, through a downpour that would threaten Noah's ark. Consequently, our backup plan of morning Bingo was activated. Also, the indoor pool, sauna, and steam room would probably get much more use than usual. When the weather warms enough and the outdoor pool is open, we keep it open on rainy days as long as nobody hears thunder or sees lightning. In a way, it's rather fun to go swimming in the rain as long as the air or water isn't too cold. Of course, the small beach at the lake is open year-round, but I don't think any members of the polar bear club have ever shown up to use it in the off season.

Several other local resorts have installed water parks, some indoor for all-year-round use, but we hadn't bit the bullet yet on that expense. However, our clientele tends to be a bit older and more sedate—few kids—so we probably don't suffer too much loss of business for that reason.

I happened to be walking through the lobby when a black Lincoln SUV pulled under the portico. It was trailed by a second identical vehicle. A man got out of the second SUV and walked completely around the first one, looking carefully in all directions before finally opening the rear door of that vehicle. A gray-haired man, about medium height and maybe sixty years old or so with a swarthy complexion, got out while another, younger-looking man, exited the far side. Both men were wearing perfectly cut, dark suits. The man who had opened the door entered the lobby first, looked around, decided neither Sandy nor I looked threatening, and motioned for the other two men to follow him. I noticed another man get out of the second vehicle and bring up the rear. The men in front and back were probably what Lauren had called the enforcers, but at least they weren't carrying violin cases or whatever are used to secrete modern machine guns. I suspected, though, that their well-made suit jackets concealed equally lethal weapons. I had no particular interest in finding out.

I decided the older man was probably Papa Guido. The man who'd been riding with him had black, wavy hair and was very tall and broad-shouldered, built like a linebacker. He wasn't actually carrying the train of the older man, but you could tell by his demeanor that he was the subservient one of the two.

The man in the lead went to the desk. "Mr. Corsana is here for his rooms," I heard him say. Normally, I would have made some excuse to hover in the lobby to hear more, much as I had done during Marvin's arrival, but something about this group suggested I probably would be better making myself scarce. Because it was that dead time between Bingo and lunch, I went to my office, grabbed my umbrella—by now the heavens had opened and it was raining catfish and eels—and sloshed my way to the cottage.

"Your father has arrived," I said to Lauren, who was once again sitting on my sofa while Johnny played on the floor with Snickers. They'd mostly been hanging out at the cottage although occasionally they disappeared to wherever. Pete had tried to explain it to me, but it sounded something like a limbo, almost a dreamless sleep, from which they'd emerge into a waking state. Apparently, ghosts don't get tired, but they seem to sleep of sorts at least some of the time.

"It's raining outside," Lauren said while staring out the window at the downpour.

"Yeah, but you'll find you won't get wet, so maybe you'll want to go at least to see your father. There's a man with him, too, a really tall guy built like a bull."

"That's probably my husband. He's not called Big John for nothing."

"Well, whoever he is, he's big. After I make a potty stop, I'll walk back up to the lodge with you, and you can check out the newcomers while I grab some lunch. They'll probably be up on the fifth floor in rooms 505 and 506. You won't be able to use the elevators unless somebody else is there to push the buttons and is going up to five, but you can use the stairs and it won't tire you out. Then you can walk right through the doors into the rooms."

"But they won't be able to see us."

"Not unless they can see ghosts. That's highly unlikely."

"Should I take Johnny with me?"

"That's up to you. However, he might get upset because his daddy and grandpa won't pay him the least bit of attention. He can stay here and hang out with Snickers or take a nap or whatever if you prefer."

"Yes, that might be best."

** ** **

"There's a man on five with a gun," Sal Aviedo said as I encountered him in the staff hallway on my way to the employee dining room. Sal is our regular security guard.

"Yeah, he's probably part of the Philadelphia mob."

"The mob. Who?"

"Does the name Guido Corsana ring a bell?" Sal's name sounds Italian, but I really knew nothing about his heritage.

"Oh God! Not him. Yeah, I know of him. Is he here?"

"Him and Big John Capobianco."

"I think I'll avoid the fifth floor."

"How about security for the other guests up there?"

"With Papa Guido and his goons on five, none of them needs to worry about outsiders bothering them."

"But how about the goons bothering them?"

"They're okay as long as nobody threatens Papa Guido."

"Which I doubt any of the other guests will do."

"They'd better not. What are those guys doing here, anyway?"

"I really don't know." I wasn't about to tell him that Guido's daughter and grandson were hanging around as ghosts after being killed in the wreck at the base of our dam. Sal doesn't know about my abilities, and I'm just as glad he doesn't. If the state police want to fill him in about what they know, that's up to them. I know we haven't been informed officially about the names of the deceased, but apparently Papa Guido and Big John have been, or they wouldn't have darkened our door.

I continued on my way to lunch and nearly collided with Marvelous Marvin who came steaming around a corner. "Oops, sorry," I apologized. He gave me a dirty look and continued storming along the hallway toward the lobby. After looking after him for a moment, I turned toward the dining room and nearly collided with George who came tooling around the same corner. At least he didn't look like an angry T-rex chasing down a helpless brontosaurus.

"What's with the racing about?" I asked. "Marvin nearly ran over me, too."

"Yeah, he said he's going up to five to have it out with Corsana and his crew. I think he wants to kick them out of those suites."

"That doesn't sound like a good idea. Have you seen those guys?"

"Not yet. Why?"

"Sal just told me there's a goon with a gun patrolling the fifth-floor hallway."

George got a sudden hopeful look. "Maybe he'll shoot Marvin."

"No such luck. Marvin will probably try to hire him away from Papa Guido."

"Yeah, and with my luck, he'll probably succeed." It's sad when your boss looks like he just attended the funeral of his best friend.

** ** **

By the time I finished lunch, a rather limp hamburger in an equally limp bun along with somewhat soggy fries, the rain had stopped, the sun was breaking through the clouds, and the animals probably were departing from the ark, still two by two. I often wondered about that Bible story. Did Noah take the fish in goldfish bowls, or did he leave them to fend for themselves?

I had a meeting at one-thirty with Cathy to plan some new activities. She had come up with some ideas to supplement the Bingo games, and we wanted to review them. I headed for her office.

"Did you hear about the man on five, the one with the gun?" was the first thing she said when I entered her office.

"Yeah, it's one of Papa Guido's henchmen."

"Papa Guido?"

"He's supposedly a mobster from Philly. Sal seems to know him or at least to know to avoid him."

"Oh? Is it a good thing we've become a haven for the Mafia?"

"I don't know. Have we had attention from that crowd in the past?"

"Not as far as I know. They're not allowed in the casino's hotel, or it can lose its license, so they'll stay at other places. Because we don't have a casino, we're under no such risk, so I guess they can come here."

"Is that necessarily a bad thing as long as they don't annoy the other guests?" I asked.

"No, I guess not. Still, I wonder why they're here."

I knew, but I decided I'd have a difficult time explaining to Cathy why and how I knew. It was hard enough getting George to believe in my ghost-sighting abilities. I really didn't feel like trying to tell somebody else.

On the Trail

Surprisingly, nobody had shot anybody else, at least not by Sunday afternoon, and to the best of my knowledge, Marvin hadn't hired away Papa Guido's pistol-packin' goon. (Sorry, I guess I should say "security agent.")

It was a beautiful afternoon, sunny with only a few puffy clouds in the sky, and a temperature in the low seventies. I could take weather like this all year round, although I doubt there's anywhere in the world like that.

I made my way to the stable to meet the new horses. Honey, the mare, and Spike, the gelding, were beautiful animals. Honey was colored all over like her name except for a lighter mane, and Spike was a few shades darker, probably what would be called chestnut, with a white blaze.

"Where did you find them?" I asked Lizzie. "I can't imagine anybody wanting to give up horses like these."

"Oh, there are plenty of them for sale, although I was lucky to get these two at a good price. I don't think the stable that owned them wanted to unload them, but that stable's in the process of closing because the owners are retiring, and nobody has stepped up to buy them out. Unfortunately, these were the only two from their stock worth buying. I'm supposed to go check out several more horses at different stables next week, though, so maybe I'll have a full contingent by next weekend."

"And then we can begin scheduling trail rides for our guests. I'm sure George has the advertising copy ready to put out there. He's been touting the upcoming horseback riding for several months, ever since the board approved the stable."

"I'm looking forward to it, too. I really love horses, probably because they've always been a part of my life."

"Yeah, I can see that would be a reason. Are you ready for us to take a ride?"

"I checked both horses out yesterday after they got here, riding down the forest road to the state highway and back. They don't seem at all skittish, so I'm sure we won't have problems with them."

Lizzie handed me a saddle, in good condition but obviously slightly used. "Did we get these from that stable, too?"

"Yeah, six saddles, a couple of dozen bridles, and some grooming tools. I have an order of more stuff coming soon, but these were in excellent shape and a lot cheaper than new ones." I decided George would be pleased with Lizzie's attitude. She was willing to save money wherever possible and not demand all new equipment. I was pretty sure most of our guests wouldn't mind slightly used gear although a couple probably would expect brand new. Those people exist everywhere, and they're not always the wealthiest ones.

I hadn't been on horseback for a couple of years, ever since I moved away from the family farm. Old Thunderbolt had gone to horse heaven a few months after that, so I didn't have access to an animal when I did go home for a visit. I think Aunt Gladys and Terry had a couple of riding horses on their farm, but I wasn't sure whether access to them would be available to a mere niece. The first few seconds on Honey's back took some getting used to again, but then I settled in and was fine.

For the last few years at the farm, I'd ridden Old Thunderbolt. However, he was old and slow, so it was kind of fun to be on the back of a young, slightly spirited but mostly gentle, mare who was capable of moving at more than a slow walk. Lizzie rode beside me on Spike, and neither horse seemed to be trying to show his or her superiority by outpacing the other. I supposed the fact they'd been associates at their former stable was a factor, so it would be interesting to find out how they'd get along with new stock.

We took the forest road all the way to the state highway, first at a walk and then at a trot, which is by far the most uncomfortable gait for the rider. Riding at a trot for any distance can leave the rider with a bruised butt. When we reached the gate at the end of the forest road, we stopped.

"Do you think they'd be okay on the paved road? It's only about a quarter mile to the lane back to the pond."

"Yeah, they should be fine as long as we don't have to deal with a lot of traffic. They were used to trail rides at their former stable, and I know they had to use some roads with cars on them."

"Mm, then let's go."

None of the roads immediately adjacent to Mountain Woods is heavily traveled. In fact, I suspect the resort generates most of the traffic. Consequently, we were passed by only a couple of cars before we reached the lane back to where the trailer had been located. I was about to turn onto it when Lizzie asked, "Where does this highway go if we follow it?"

"Eventually up to the casino, but that's several miles. However, there's a narrower road that cuts off to the left in a couple of hundred yards, a shortcut of sorts. However, it's kind of winding and hilly. It's the one that passes the base of our dam."

"Mm. I'd like to get off the road, now, but maybe sometime we can head that way, although if it's too narrow, it might be difficult to avoid cars."

"Yeah, it might." I pointed along the unpaved lane toward where the trailer had once stood. "This will take us to the trailer site and the pond." I turned Honey's head in that direction and gently kicked my heels against her flanks. As she started ambling along, I decided I'd have to invest in some cowboy boots, boot-cut jeans, and hat. If I was going to be leading trail rides, I'd want to dress accordingly.

We'd gone about a hundred feet or so at a walk when I noticed a trail leading off to the right. In all my walking, I hadn't really taken this lane all the way to the state highway. I'd driven it numerous times in my car, but when one is driving, one is supposed to pay attention to the road and not the scenery. Okay, I often cheat and admire the scenery, but here it was lucky I paid attention to the road because I usually had something else on my mind, one of those evil distractions that lead to accidents.

"Where does that path go?" Lizzie asked.

"Damned if I know. I never noticed it until now." Detectives are supposed to be keenly aware of their surroundings. Maybe I should reconsider opening my own agency.

"Let's follow it a ways and see," Lizzie said.

She moved into the lead and turned onto the path, which was quite narrow at the beginning where it crossed a small meadow but then widened to about four feet when it entered the trees on the far side.

The meadow had been full of colorful butterflies fluttering between assorted spring wildflowers, and now, as we entered the wooded area, birds were singing all around us, a rabbit hopped across the trail ahead, and several squirrels were chirruping from nearby branches. If I had to describe the moment, the word "idyllic" comes to mind.

The first trees we encountered were a clump of sumacs with their fuzzy spring shoots and tiny red leaves just beginning to open. Almost the first trees to leaf out in this area, in a few days their leaves would turn green, and then their fruit clusters would start to appear.

We rode for a while, maybe a quarter mile or so, as the trail slowly mounted a hill. On the way we threaded our way through clusters of hemlocks, the Pennsylvania state tree, that pushed their soft green branches out over the trail. We rounded a bend and found ourselves at a paved road, with the trail continuing on the far side.

"Where the heck are we?" Lizzie asked.

"I'm not sure, but I think this is that road that passes our dam," I said. "Yeah, there's no other road that goes this way before that one, so it must be."

"Do you want to cross over and try that other trail?"

"Why not?" I'm nosy, as you may recall from my former adventures, so I was game.

After carefully looking both ways for traffic—this was a surprisingly good spot because I remembered most of this road as having a lot of curves and hills that restricted visibility—we continued into the woods on the far side of the road. Another few hundred yards on, I noticed boot prints at a spot on the trail that was bare dirt. I remembered that everything had been wet the night of the accident, but since then we'd had no rain, so these tracks had to be from about that time or earlier because the ground was too hard now for shoes to sink in.

"I wonder..." I said as I dismounted and handed the reins to Lizzie.

"What's wrong?" she asked. "Did Honey pick up a stone or something?"

"No, she's fine. I just want to check out these prints."

"Why? I'm sure people use this trail at least occasionally because otherwise it would get overgrown fairly quickly."

"Yeah, it would. It's just a thought I had." Again, I wasn't ready to tell Lizzie I was looking for the guy who'd carjacked a woman who was now a ghost. If he'd still been in the car when it rolled down the embankment, he probably had been thrown clear, and with no body in the area, he'd obviously survived and been able to get away. While I had no way of being certain these tracks were made by him, the absence of any others in the hardened dirt and the timing of the last time the soil had been wet enough certainly implied it.

Lizzie pulled her phone from her shirt pocket and looked at it. "Hm, no signal. Is that a common problem around here?"

"Yeah, unfortunately. We're still living in the dark ages in some parts of the Poconos."

"Well, my phone says it's going on four. Shouldn't we be heading back for dinner?"

I took Honey's reins, grabbed the saddle horn, put my sneakered foot into the stirrup, and hoisted myself into the saddle. "Yeah, but do you mind if we ride just a little bit farther? They'll have food out on the buffet line until seven."

"Okay, but I'd really like to get back before then."

"No problemo. Just a couple of hundred yards more, and then back home. It really won't take all that long. We can even open up to a gallop on the last leg."

"Yeah, that would be fun. I tried it yesterday with each horse, and they both performed well."

Tracking and Talking

Until now, I didn't recall seeing any footprints on bare spots on the trail—spots in areas heavily shaded by evergreens because the deciduous trees were just beginning to leaf out—which kind of suggested that the walker, whoever he or she was, had joined the trail at this point. Of course, I hadn't been looking for footprints, so it was possible I'd missed them. I did look at the surrounding brush to see whether anybody could have walked through it, but the weedy growth that would later fill in the sunnier spots had yet to appear, and any leftovers from last season were too crushed by winter snowfalls to show much. The spaces between evergreens such as hemlocks, other pines, and rhododendrons seldom had that weedy growth, especially where they were almost perpetually deprived of sunlight, but it would take some close examination of the ground to locate tracks, and today I simply didn't have the time. Also, I wanted to go a bit farther today just to see whether the tracks I'd already discovered led anywhere.

We continued along the trail for probably another half-mile, and the footprints we were following continued. Their pattern was strange in that the spacing wasn't even, as it would be if the person had been walking steadily or running. In fact, the right print was only slightly ahead of the left print. "What do you make of that?" I asked.

"I'd say this sucker was limping. Also, judging from the size of those prints, I'm pretty sure we're tracking a man."

"It's a shame we don't have one of the natives with us who used to populate this area. He probably could have told you the age, height, and weight of the person, too."

Lizzie laughed. "And what he had for breakfast."

"I wonder where this trail goes."

"You'd think we'd have come upon another road by now."

"Lizzie, you haven't spent a lot of time around here, have you?"

"No, not too much. Why?"

"It's amazing how far you can go in some areas around here without crossing a road except maybe for a dirt one going to some hunter's cabin. Google the area and look at the satellite views."

"Which I can't do now because I don't have any signal."

"No. I think you'd be able to get the GPS coordinates because those come from the satellites, but you'd need a signal to get the map."

"Okay, Three-Zee, do you mind if we head back? The clock on my phone still runs even without a signal."

"Yes, of course. However, do you mind if I borrow Honey tomorrow afternoon? I must lead a hike in the morning, but I want to follow that track farther before we get rain that could wash it away."

"Yeah, sure. You know where the tack is stored, and I'm sure Honey won't complain."

We had turned around by now and were returning to the resort. This time I watched to see if there were any footprints between where I'd first spotted them and the paved road. There were none.

** ** **

Bambi was able to join us for dinner, and afterward Bambi and I returned to the cottage while Lizzie went to her room to make some phone calls. She said she'd join us later.

When we entered the cottage, Pete was sprawled on the sofa. "I wish I could figure out a way to turn on the TV," he complained. "Sometimes I get kind of bored just sitting here."

"Hey, even if we left the TV on for you, you'd probably want to switch channels at some point," I said. "Besides, I thought you said ghosts don't get bored."

"Well, we don't, actually. We sort of hibernate or nap or whatever, which kills time very well."

"So, there's your answer. Anyway, have you seen Lauren or little Johnny lately?"

"I know they went up to the lodge earlier to hang around with Lauren's father and husband, so I don't know whether they're coming back tonight."

"We are and we have," a female voice said as Lauren walked into the living room through the front door.

"Where's Snickers?" Johnny asked as he followed her into the room.

"I'm not sure," I said. "You go look for him."

"Okay," Johnny said and ran into the kitchen.

By now, Bambi had settled on the couch next to Pete, and I had plopped into the easy chair. I was glad for the cushioned upholstery instead of the hard chairs in the employee dining room because my butt definitely hadn't been prepared for this afternoon's pounding, especially the trotting.

"Lauren, I think I've discovered something about your carjacker," I said to the woman after she'd taken a seat on the arm of the sofa.

"Oh, what's that?"

"I think he was still in the car with you when it rolled down the hill, and he was thrown free."

"I guess that makes sense, but wouldn't it be possible he'd already had me drop him off somewhere?"

"Yes, it's possible, but I found some evidence this afternoon that leads me to believe otherwise. I found some tracks in the woods near where you went off the road of some man-sized boots."

"Couldn't that be anybody? There seem to be a lot of hikers around here."

"Yes, but they're in a stretch of trail that would have been muddy the night of the accident, and the man was limping. The tracks were too sharply etched to have been made before the rain, and it's been dry since, so tracks that deep would have had to be made soon after the rain stopped."

"It wasn't raining when he carjacked me. That's true. But it had been raining quite hard a short time earlier. I don't recall that the rain started up again while he was in the car with me."

"So, now all I have to do is follow those tracks and see where they lead. Bam, what time do you get off tomorrow afternoon?"

""Two. Why?"

"Are you up to taking a horseback ride?"

"Sure. I haven't been on a horse in a couple of years, and I really miss it."

"Okay. I have the afternoon off, too, so meet me at the stable as soon as you can, and we'll go tracking."

"Will Lizzie mind? After all, those are more-or-less her horses."

"Actually, they're the resort's horses, and technically I am sort of her boss, but I already asked her, and she said she'll be tied up but has no problem with me taking the horse out."

"Did you ask her about me?"

"No, but I'm authorizing it."

Bambi grinned. "It's nice to be a close friend of the boss."

"Do you mind if I join you?" Lauren asked.

"Well, I don't have a horse for you, plus I'm not sure how you could control one even if I did, but if you're willing to run alongside, come along."

"Me, too?" Pete asked.

"Of course. Besides, how could I stop you?"

Pete grinned. "You can't. This being a ghost has some advantages."

"Do you mind if I leave Johnny here to play with Snickers?" Lauren asked.

"No, as long as Snickers says it's okay. However, wouldn't you like to leave him with his father?"

"What good would that do? Neither my husband nor my father can see him or know he's with them, so they're liable to go off somewhere and leave him just sitting there confused. He's only three. It was hard enough telling him today why they wouldn't pay attention to him."

"Yes, I see your point. Hm, I just thought of something. Some animals seem to be able to see or at least sense ghosts. What will happen if you spook the horses?"

"If we do, we'll just hang back far enough that they won't know we're following," Pete said. "Besides, not all animals can see me. I don't seem to bother the bunnies and birds."

"No, nor the seagulls on the beach. Maybe, like Bambi and me, Snickers is an anomaly."

"Don't forget that girl in Ocean City you mentioned, the high school kid from last fall, and Jason." Jason was the Chatham, Massachusetts cop I'd met while on Cape Cod. He'd paid me a visit last fall during the Haunted Woods event, and we were keeping in touch by phone and video chat, but we hadn't been able to work out a time for another get-together.

"Yeah, Jason probably would be a big help right now. After all, he is a trained detective. There's also that little boy near where I was staying temporarily in the cabin."

"Him, too, so there really are a number of people who can see and talk to me."

"But percentage-wise, not a lot."

"No, not a lot."

Looking for Clues

Bambi showed up at the stable at about twenty past two, having run down to the cottage after work to change from her kitchen whites into jeans, sweatshirt, and sneakers. She agreed that we'd have to invest in more appropriate garb for trail riding although she said she had stuff at her parents' home that would work, including boots and hat. I vaguely remembered her wearing stuff like that when we went riding together back when we lived with our folks. I had had boots and hat, too, but the hat had been crushed by my brother, Joe, and my feet had grown another size since I had worn the boots.

We got the horses saddled fairly quickly considering we hadn't done it for a couple of years. However, there is such a thing as muscle memory, so if you don't think about something, you'll often find you can still do it.

Last evening at dinner Lizzie and I had gone into details about our tracking adventure, so I didn't have to explain about where we were going or why. Of course, Lizzie still didn't know why I was so interested in a set of random footprints, but I had explained it away by saying I wanted to practice following somebody just as an experiment.

Lauren and Pete had come to the stable with Bambi. Honey seemed to notice them but didn't seem to care, and Spike paid no attention to them at all. At least my fears about the ghosts spooking the horses hadn't materialized.

Because ghosts don't get tired or even winded if they run, the two trotted along behind us as we walked and then trotted our horses, first along the forest road, and then along the trail to the trailer site. We increased the pace to a canter as we started along the lane from the trailer site to the new trail I'd discovered, but slowed back to a walk to allow Pete and Lauren to catch up. They may not have tired, but they still couldn't run faster than living folks.

It was another beautiful day, and we had decided we'd forego dinner if necessary to follow the tracks farther. In late April sunset is approaching eight p.m. because we're in daylight saving time by then. That means we had until after eight-thirty until it became too dark to see. Also, we had our own vehicles back at the resort, and there was always McDonald's if we missed dinner.

We crossed the road and followed the trail until we reached the first footprints. This time we both dismounted and studied the surrounding brush. Eventually I found some tracks that seemed to be coming from the direction of the dam, so we remounted and continued along the trail past where Lizzie and I had turned around.

So far, the tracks seemed to be following the trail, and their spacing was consistent with somebody limping. In fact, the tracks were growing closer together as if the person was slowing down.

"Maybe his leg was hurting more," I said. "He definitely seems to be walking more slowly."

"You're right. I wonder if he was walking in the dark all this way, or if it was starting to get light."

"Hard to tell because we have no way of knowing when he set off. We're assuming he got moving right after being thrown from the car, but he could have lain there for a while, maybe even unconscious. Remember, I didn't actually find the wreck until much later in the morning. Lauren, do you have any idea what time you might have had your wreck?"

"Well, like I said, I was carjacked around midnight or maybe a little later—I never checked the time. I don't know how long it would take to drive from there to here, but I do know I didn't stop anywhere after he got in the car, so unless I stopped after the point where my memory fades, it couldn't have taken more than a half hour to get to where I crashed."

"No, that sounds about right. If he got moving right away, he'd have been walking in darkness for several hours because it doesn't start to get light until sometime between five and five-thirty. Of course, he could have sat and rested for a while or not even started walking until much later."

"Does it matter?"

"Probably not. He was already gone by the time I discovered the wreck, and you and Johnny were still in limbo somewhere, so there's no way we'll ever find out unless we catch him and he tells us."

"Which doesn't seem likely," Pete said.

"Stranger things have happened."

We were traveling at a walk because a higher speed might have caused us to lose sight of the tracks or miss some other clue. As it was, I almost missed where the footprints turned off the trail into a grassy area and then emerged a few feet farther along. Bambi was the one who spotted it.

Bambi and I quickly dismounted, and all four of us studied the prints. "It looks like he was beginning to drag his right leg," Bambi said. Then we headed into the grass to see whether he had rested or left some other clue.

"Look at this," Lauren said from the far side of the area where a clump of dead weeds bordered the grass, which was now greening up nicely because of the warm weather.

I went over to her to see a piece of white cloth on the ground, or at least it had been a piece of white cloth, probably a handkerchief, but now it was mostly dark red. Bambi came up beside me. "Looks like dried blood," she said.

I bent over to pick it up, but Bambi belted me on the arm before I could touch it. "Hey! What was that all about?"

"DNA. You were about to contaminate it."

"Oh yeah. Sorry. So how are we supposed to get this back to the resort."

"Simple." Bambi fumbled in her jeans pocket for a moment. "Damned things must be shrinking."

"Or maybe you've been tasting too much while you're cooking."

"Yeah, that, too. Okay, here it is." She pulled out a plastic bag. "Never know when you're going to need one of these."

By using a stick we broke off a nearby branch, we manipulated the blood-stained hankie into the bag and then zipped it shut.

"First evidence," I said.

"Yeah. It's a shame we don't have any plaster of Paris to make a cast of the footprints."

"You don't have any of that in your pocket, do you?" Bambi gave me a dirty look, so I assumed she didn't.

"Do you think one of us could come out here tomorrow and make a cast?"

"Maybe, if it doesn't rain before then."

"I know, we can run into town tonight and pick up a bag. Walmart should have some. Then I can drive over here tomorrow—I noticed a wide spot where I can pull off the road to park—and make a cast. I can do it during my lunch hour. If I remember right, that plaster dries pretty quickly."

"Don't forget water, something to mix the plaster in, and plastic bags to carry the casts after they dry."

"Yeah, yeah, I will. I'm not a total idiot, you know." I glanced at Pete who was grinning at me. "Shut up, Pete!" I snapped before he could get in the insult I'm sure he was planning.

After some careful searching we pulled up some grass that appeared to be bloodstained and tucked it into another plastic bag Bambi pulled from her pocket. "How many of those to you have?" I asked.

"One more, so we'd better not find too many more clues."

"Or at least clues that need bagging."

We remounted our horses and continued to follow the trail. The footprints were very close together and wandered all over the path. After another hundred yards or so, they stopped at a narrow grass strip that bordered the path.

We studied the area carefully. At least there was no dead body lying nearby although I suspected Lauren probably wouldn't have minded very much if we'd found one. We saw what looked like more dried blood on the grass, but we decided not to collect it, figuring we had more than enough DNA samples. Also, this would leave our remaining bag free in case we found something else worth collecting. After careful study of the dirt on the trail just beyond that point, we found some very shallow footprints, somewhat scuffed and hard to read.

"It looks like he must have rested here for quite a while, at least until the mud dried somewhat, or these prints would be deeper," I said.

"Should we ride farther?" Bambi asked.

"Maybe another quarter mile or so, but it'll be difficult to see where he might have gone since those prints are so weak."

"Yeah, okay." Again, we remounted and followed the trail. Occasionally, we could make out a footprint or two, but they were getting weaker and weaker. I noticed, too, that the sun was dropping pretty far toward the horizon.

"Bam, I think we'd better head back. I'd rather not be out here after dark on unfamiliar trails. Besides, Lizzie might be in panic if the horses aren't back by a reasonable hour."

"Can't you call her?"

I checked my phone. "Not unless we use smoke signals. No signal."

"Still, I wonder how far this trail goes."

"Well, it must go somewhere. It's too wide and worn to be just a game trail."

"I can help," Pete said.

"What do you mean?"

"I've been talking it over with Lauren, and we agreed I should continue on. I won't get cold or tired, I can see better in the dark than you can, and even though I can't do much if I do find something or somebody, at least I can come back and tell you about it."

"Pete, you're a godsend. I could kiss you."

"Hey, no making out with my boyfriend," Bambi snapped. "He's mine. You go find your own."

I glanced at Lauren who seemed to be trying to decide whether to break out in hysterical laughter or try to figure out some way to have Bambi committed. I could understand her dilemma.

It was an hour later and the reddening sun was just perched on the horizon when we finally reached the stable where we found Lizzie pacing nervously at the big, open doors. "You two scared the crap out of me," she complained. "I was all ready to call 911."

"And tell them what? I'm not sure they have a mounted patrol that could go out looking for us, and even if they do, we probably have to be gone more than a couple of hours."

"Yeah, you're right. Still, the horses are my responsibility, so I don't want anything to happen to them." As we spoke, Bambi and I were busily removing saddles and bridles. We hadn't been riding fast so the horses didn't need drying off, but I was certain Lizzie would make sure they were probably fed and groomed. I could tell that the girl loved horses.

As Bambi and I turned to leave, Lizzie said, "Oh, I almost forgot. Some guy was snooping around here when I got back here earlier."

"Oh, who?"

"He never did say his name, but he was a skinny little twerp, about your height, I guess, and half bald. Mean SOB."

"Sounds like Marvelous Marvin."

"Oh yeah, that owner you mentioned. Is he going to be around here all the time?"

"I hope not. He only shows up about once a year for a couple of weeks and drives everybody crazy."

"Well, if you hear of a guy being stomped to death for tormenting a horse, he'll be here in one of the stables."

"You'll probably get a thank-you note from George, maybe even a promotion and raise."

Plaster Prints

Monday evening Bambi and I made a run into town to pick up some plaster of Paris, a couple of plastic containers, some bottles of water, and a box of extra-large plastic bags with zipper seals. I was pretty sure casts of those footprints wouldn't fit into a normal gallon-size bag, and it turned out I was right.

Tuesday morning dawned cloudy. I checked the weather forecast on my phone, and the afternoon forecast called for showers. I hoped they'd hold off until I was able to get a cast of at least one or two of the better prints.

My morning schedule was full because I had to lead a hike around the lake, which meant I couldn't get away to do my casts until lunchtime. Fortunately, the rain had held off.

I loaded my supplies into my car and headed off toward where I could get onto the trail where we'd discovered the footprints. The regular paved access to the lodge came in from the other side from the forest road, so it was a several mile drive that brought me in past the dam face where Lauren had gone off the road. I could see that a swerve at that point—the guard rail had failed to do its duty and was bent and crushed—could send one careening down the hill, not a trip I wanted to take. I slowed almost to a stop when I noticed that somebody was down at the creek. However, when that person turned and stared up the hill at me, I decided to get out of there. It could have been one of Papa Guido's goons, they were armed, and I didn't want this one using me for target practice.

At the wide spot next to the trail, I was able to get the car just off the paved area where it wouldn't be a hazard or get me a ticket. Then I had about a quarter mile walk to where we'd discovered the first clear print. As soon as I reached it, I mixed the plaster in one of the plastic containers with some of the bottled water and then poured it into two of the best prints, one of each foot.

I waited nervously for the plaster to set enough to move, which took a good hour. I had lugged along the small folding spade I keep in my trunk to dig me out of snowdrifts, so when the plaster looked firm enough, I carefully worked the spade beneath one of the prints and plaster and then slid the whole mess into a bag. I did the same with the other print, just as a light rain began falling.

Now I had a bit of a dilemma because I had to carry the bag with my supplies and trash, the spade, and the two bags of footprints, trying to be as careful as possible so I wouldn't break the casts. I made it to the car with both casts in one piece, but shortly after I began my walk the heavens opened up, so I was drenched by the time I got there. I put the casts on the back floor where they could lie flat, the other stuff in the trunk, and crawled into the driver's seat. My seats aren't leather or vinyl, so I was pretty sure it would take them a while to dry out from contact with my wet butt.

I made it back to the lodge okay, drove down to my cottage, and took the casts inside. After changing into dry clothing, I moved my car to the employee lot and headed inside to my office where I had to get ready to host an afternoon Bingo game. I had to forego lunch, but Pete keeps hinting—no, make that blatantly insisting—that I'm putting on weight and should cut down on calories. Of course, I'd probably eat twice as much at dinner just to make up for it.

** ** **

"So, what do we do with them?" Bambi asked as she stared at the casts after we'd returned to the cottage after dinner.

"I'm not sure. I think the police would like to know about them, but how do I explain things to them? As far as they know, Lauren lost control of her car and tumbled down that hill. They know nothing about a carjacking or a person of interest escaping through those woods."

"Yeah, I can see where that's going to be tough. You never told Liz you can see ghosts, did you?"

"Of course not. I mean, did you really believe me all those years before you could see them, too?"

"At first, I wasn't sure, but you seemed to know too much about a couple of things that you'd have had no way of knowing if you hadn't talked to a ghost. By the way, speaking of ghosts, have you seen any of them around here today?"

"No, not since yesterday. Okay, little Johnny was here this afternoon when I got back with the plaster casts. He was playing with Snickers. I haven't seen him since, though."

"That's odd. I didn't see Pete up at the kitchen, either. Usually he's hanging around getting in my way."

"Oh, I'm here," Pete said while fading into view. "I'd never run out on Bambi."

"Mm," Bambi said. "So, where have you been?"

"Do I detect just a trace of jealousy in your voice, my love? Fear not. Lauren isn't my type. Anyway, I believe she and her brat are up in the lodge bothering her husband and father."

I decided to intervene. "What did you find out yesterday? When I left you, you were hot on the trail of the carjacker."

"Yes, I was that. I followed the tracks, which were rapidly becoming weaker, for about another half mile. It looked like the person had stopped several times to rest. Finally, they ended at a cabin."

Readers may wonder at the proliferation of woodland cabins in my stories, but such are very common in the Pocono Mountain region. Some are hunters' cabins, used mostly during those seasons; some are vacation homes, used for that purpose; and some are full-time dwellings. Many are on unpaved roads deep in the wilderness.

"I assume you went inside," I said.

"Of course. You told me to follow the guy. You didn't tell me when to stop."

"And…"

"Okay, he's now deceased."

Bambi looked at him in shock. "You didn't kill him, did you?"

"Of course not. How would I have pulled that off?"

"Did he bleed out from the leg injury?" I asked.

"While I'm sure he lost a lot of blood from that particular injury, I think the bullet hole in his head was more likely the actual cause of death."

"Bullet hole… in his head?"

"Yeah, one of those."

"How the heck did that happen?"

"Well, first you take a gun, either rifle or pistol—it wasn't a shotgun or AR-15 because the injuries from those are rather obvious—lots of holes—and then you aim it at the person, either intentionally or accidentally. Finally, you pull the trigger. Voila! Bullet hole."

I stuck out my tongue at him.

"Oh, and the body was starting to decompose a bit. The maggots in his mouth kind of implied that."

Bambi grimaced. "Gross. You didn't have to give us that detail."

"No, I was merely alerting you to the fact that you probably don't want to go in there unprepared. I'm sure this warmish weather has made things worse."

"So, why did it take you more than twenty-four hours to come back here and tell us?" I asked.

"Well, I took the long way around, using the dirt road to that cabin and then several other roads. That trail was merely an alternate route and certainly not wide enough for cars. Also, he probably isn't going anywhere—the cabin doors are closed and latched, so critters aren't going to get in to clean up—so I wasn't in any particular hurry."

"Pete, sometimes you drive me crazy. How the heck am I going to give this information to the police?"

"Well, first you touch various places on the screen of your phone, and then you…"

"Shut up, Pete!" I turned to my best friend. "Bam, do you think we should find this cabin and check it out?"

"I guess I'd rather not because I'm sure the body has acquired a less-than-pleasant odor, but I suppose we should. Still, I'm not sure how we could tell the cops. I mean, why would we be checking out that cabin."

"Hm. Good point. I guess we could say we saw the footprints and blood, and eventually we decided to investigate farther and discovered the body."

** ** **

Pete rode with us in Bambi's old truck, which we chose because it had a higher undercarriage, and we weren't sure about the condition of the dirt access road. By now it was almost totally dark, so we had opted to take along the cheap helmet lights we had purchased for exploring a corn maze last fall. The darned things worked surprisingly well, so we had kept them just for occasions like this.

All was dark and mostly quiet when we parked outside the cabin. It's rather surprising how many sounds one hears in a remote woodland at night, especially in spring and summer. The crickets hadn't yet started their perpetual mating songs, and it was too early for cicadas, but some spring frogs were making noises, and there are always various nocturnal birds. An owl was hooting in a nearby tree, either calling to a mate or bragging about its latest dinner of raw rodent.

As the truck engine crackled and popped while it began to cool, we stepped out of the vehicle, switched on our headlamps, and made our way to the cabin. Fortunately, nobody challenged us because I'm sure I would have soiled my undies if they had.

The cabin door was closed and latched but not locked. I turned the knob and pushed the door open, and Bambi and I both gagged. Pete didn't gag, but he was right. The body was no longer in the best of condition.

After we got our stomachs more or less under control, we walked to the body of a man lying on the floor. His eyes were open and staring at the open rafters above, but they were well beyond seeing anything. He looked to be around forty, plus or minus a few years, with blond hair and just the beginning of a stubble on his chin and upper lip. This description matched what Lauren had told us about her kidnapper.

"Do you think we should call Liz now or at least 911?" Bambi asked.

"No, not yet. I think we should wait until we're back at our cottage and call Liz's cell phone. We can tell her we saw the tracks yesterday before the rain, noticed the blood, and finally decided to call after thinking about it for a while. We won't tell her we entered the cabin and found the body."

"Did we leave any prints or DNA?"

"I'll wipe the door latch, but I think that's the only thing we touched." I looked at the floor. "I don't see any footprints we might have left, so we should be okay there."

"Yes, it's good the area outside is covered with gravel. I wonder who owns this cabin."

"Does it matter?"

"Probably not to us."

Six Impossible Things

We did as I had suggested and waited until we got back to our cottage before calling Liz Heyer's cell phone. I had her number from dealing with her at last fall's Haunted Woods. Besides, I'd checked my phone at the cabin, and we were definitely in a dead area for signal.

"Why didn't you call 911 or at least call me sooner?" Liz complained. "I'm not on duty now, but I can call it in."

"We weren't sure, and I didn't want to be accused of wasting police time, but the more I thought about those blood stains I began to worry that the hiker might have been seriously hurt. Anyway, I saw them this morning when we took a ride up that trail before the rain started." I neglected to mention that I had actually seen the blood stains nearly twenty-four hours earlier and the footprints about twenty-four hours before that.

"Well, we'll check it out, but that rain probably washed away most of the blood stains. I'll let you know if we find anything."

"Thanks, Liz. I owe you." Yes, I did, but exactly how I could repay her I had no idea.

"How about Lizzie?" Bambi asked after I'd disconnected.

"What do you mean, Lizzie? I just talked to her. Oh, *our* Lizzie. Yeah, she was with me when I first discovered the footprints. I think we'd better have a chat with her. Hopefully, she'll play along."

"Let me see whether she's in her room. I think this might require a face-to-face."

"I think you're right."

** ** **

Lizzie was in her room but so was her roommate, so Lizzie agreed to meet us in the lounge. There's a table in an alcove that is far enough away from others and the bar that softly spoken conversations can't be easily overheard. Also, there's always some kind of background music, either recorded or, occasionally, live that tends to mask private conversations. She had already managed to snag that table by the time Bambi and I arrived with Pete following us.

"What's up?" she asked.

"We have to talk about something," I said. "Do you remember following those footprints the other day?"

"Of course. I'm not senile yet."

"No, it's just that we'd sort of like you to forget about them."

"What do you mean?"

"Okay, Bambi and I followed them much farther and found blood stains when the prints started to show that the walker was weakening."

"Blood stains? Do you mean the person was injured?"

"Well, yeah, but it gets worse."

"Okay, how worse?"

"Tonight, we drove out there and found the body of the hiker in a cabin."

"Ouch! He must have been pretty badly injured if he bled out."

"There are arteries in the legs that can cause that, but that wasn't how he died."

"Yes, the femoral arteries, but how did he die if he didn't bleed out?"

"The bullet hole in the middle of his forehead was probably the reason."

Lizzie turned pale. "The b-bullet hole? You did say bullet hole."

"Yes, I'm afraid I did."

"Three-Zee, Bambi, what the heck's going on here?"

"Oh, it's really nothing to do with you, actually nothing really to do with any of us, but it has a lot to do with the burnt-out wreck we found below the dam."

"No, there's something here you're not telling me, yet I think I should know about."

"Okay, I'll tell you, but you probably won't believe me. You might wish you had that axe you didn't use on your mother and father to use on Bambi and me."

"Mm. I've been able to believe six impossible things before breakfast—that's from *Alice in Wonderland*—so try me."

"Bambi and I have been talking to the ghosts of the woman and boy who died in that wreck."

Lizzie had been sipping her gin and tonic, and she choked. After she stopped coughing, she said, "You what?"

"Sorry, but I mean it. We've been talking to their ghosts. In fact, I think they're upstairs right now with the woman's father and husband."

"The mobsters?"

"Yeah, them."

"You're right. This is almost beyond *Alice in Wonderland*. How is it I haven't seen them?"

"Because you can't see or hear ghosts."

"How do you know?"

"Because Pete is standing next to you making faces and disgusting noises, and you haven't noticed him at all."

"Who the hell is Pete?"

"Well, he is, or I guess I should say was, George's stepson. He was shot down along the forest road about two years ago, right after Bambi and I started working here."

"Oh, does that mean everybody who ever died here is still hanging around?"

"No, not at all. Most ghosts move on as soon as they learn how they died and, in the case of murder, who killed them."

"Move on?"

"To somewhere, somehow. I really don't know."

Lizzie looked at Bambi. "Can you see them, too?" Bambi nodded.

Lizzie gulped the rest of her drink including, I think, the remaining ice cubes. Then she frantically waved at our server. "I need another. No, bring me a straight whiskey. Make it a double.

"Okay, let's say I believe you," Lizzie continued after the server scurried off toward the bar. "If ghosts move on after they learn how they were murdered—I'm assuming this Pete guy was murdered—why is he still hanging around?"

I gulped. "Because he's Bambi's boyfriend."

Lizzie stared at Bambi. "Is this true?" Bambi looked sheepish and nodded again. "Okay, he was your boyfriend before he died, right?" Bambi shook her head. "Maybe I should have ordered a triple. No, heck, just bring me the whole bottle."

"Er, I'm sorry," I said. "I told you that you probably wouldn't believe it."

"This is probably way more than six impossible things. You're telling me that Bambi is in love with a ghost, and he's standing here beside me."

"Grinning," Bambi added.

"And there's no way I can see or hear him."

"No, well, maybe. Pete, share space with Lizzie for a moment."

Pete walked through Lizzie, and she suddenly shivered. "What the heck? Did somebody just dump a glassful of ice cubes down my back?"

"No, but Pete just walked through you and your chair. You'll feel a chill when he does that."

"I certainly did feel a chill, but it only lasted for a few seconds."

"Yeah, that's because he didn't stop while he was occupying the same space as you. If he had, you'd still feel it. It's how Bambi and he first kind of got together."

"Huh?"

"She wasn't able to see him until last summer when we were at Cape Cod. Before that she only knew him by his chill."

At that moment the waitress placed the double shot in front of Lizzie, who immediately grabbed it and tossed it down her throat. "Thanks," she said to the startled waitress, "I needed that."

"Do you want another?" the young woman asked. Cocktail servers learn to deal with all kinds of customers.

"My reeling brain says, 'Yes,' but I'd better not." The waitress nodded and headed back toward the bar.

"Is this Pete character at least good-looking?" Lizzie asked.

"Pete character?" Pete huffed.

"Shut up, Pete!" I snapped. "Yes, he's gorgeous. He was working in Hollywood and had come home for a visit when he was killed." Bambi nodded, and Pete grinned.

"That sucks," Lizzie said.

"Absolutely sucks," Pete said.

"So, what do you know about the woman who was killed in the wreck?"

"Her name's Lauren Capobianco, and she's pretty sure her husband is a hit man working for her father, Guido Corsana. Papa Guido is some sort of godfather type in the Philly area."

"Yeah, I've heard of him—nothing good, of course. Is he the one upstairs?"

"Both him and Big John Capobianco, actually, but Papa Guido's in the bridal suite."

"The bridal suite? What the heck?"

"It's okay. He's not here on his honeymoon. The décor is convertible, but it's our biggest suite."

"What about the little boy?"

"Johnny Capobianco. Mostly he's been hanging out in our cottage playing with Snickers."

"Your cat."

"Yeah, my cat."

"Who can see ghosts."

"Yeah."

"Maybe I should have that other drink."

** ** **

Lizzie was giggling when she left the table to go to her room in the employee dorm, so she probably hadn't needed that extra G and T, but she was still walking—okay, staggering a bit—without assistance. At least she wasn't a mean drunk. Bambi and I, who'd both limited ourselves to one drink apiece, walked back to our cottage without staggering.

We'd just gotten inside the door when my phone rang. The caller ID showed Liz Heyer's name.

"Hello, Liz," I answered.

"You have a lot of explaining to do."

"Why?"

"You saw the body in the cabin."

"Yes."

"And you saw the bullet hole in the forehead."

"Yes."

"You didn't happen to put the bullet hole in the forehead, did you?"

"No."

"Three-Zee, you're going to drive me to drink. I think I need to hear the whole story."

"Mm. Okay, maybe."

"No maybe about it. I'm technically off-duty, and I haven't told my colleagues the name of my informant—yet—but I need to know more."

"Yes, of course. But you'll have to believe six impossible things before breakfast."

"What?"

"Just joking. Are you planning to come over here tonight?"

"Yes, I'll be there in a few minutes. Wait up for me."

Police Involvement, Sort of

Liz showed up in about twenty minutes during which time Bambi and I changed into our warm pajamas. The night had turned chilly under a clear, moonlit sky. Meanwhile, Lauren and Johnny had returned from the lodge, and, along with Pete, Lauren was sitting with Bambi on the sofa.

"Okay, talk," Liz snapped after I'd motioned her to the easy chair. I settled my bum on the arm of the sofa because the seats were rather crowded with Bambi and two ghosts. Little Johnny and Snickers were playing on the floor. Liz looked at Snickers curiously.

"You are not going to believe this," I said.

"Try me."

"The ghost of the woman who was killed in that wreck, Lauren Capobianco, is sitting there on the sofa beside Bambi, and her little boy, Johnny, is on the floor playing with Snickers."

Liz shook her head savagely. "I thought your cat was behaving oddly, but I could swear you said he's playing with a ghost."

"He is."

"Three-Zee, I'm off-duty, I'm tired, I have to go into work at six for a twelve-hour shift, and I'm in no mood to play games. What the hell are you talking about?"

"Just what I said. I can see and talk to ghosts. Bambi can, too."

"Well, okay, you probably got the name of the dead woman and her son from her father and husband, both of whom have kind of taken over your fifth floor."

"No, Liz, I'm serious. Their ghosts are right here in this room."

"And the ghost of the dead guy, too?"

"No, not him, or at least not so far. He may show up later."

"Is this something new, your ability to see ghosts?"

"For Bambi, only about a year. For me, since I was seven."

"Oh. I assume you were chatting with the ghosts at the Haunted Woods last fall."

"Yes, or at least the real ones. Pete keeps insisting that real ghosts don't wear white sheets, and he's right. They look like normal people dressed the way they were when they died."

Liz shook her head again. Then she asked, "Pete? Who the hell is Pete?"

"Bambi's boyfriend, Pete Gardenko."

"Wait, I seem to remember hearing about a case a couple of years ago before I joined the force. It was a murder case, and the victim was George Wylie's stepson. I think that was his name."

"Yes, it was; actually still is."

"And he's Bambi's boyfriend."

"Yes."

"Bambi, are you aware that your boyfriend is dead?"

"Of course," Bambi replied. "I've known that all along."

"Oh. Okay, I'll believe you because it's easier than not believing you. However, I'm not going to mention this to anybody at the station— ever."

"Probably a good idea not to," I said.

"Are there a lot of you?"

"A lot of who?"

"People who can see ghosts."

"No, not too many."

"Around here?"

"Well, there's Tasha McGhee, the black girl who played a werewolf in the Haunted Woods, and then there's a little boy named Izzy McMahon, who lives, or at least lived, in a wooded area over near Mount Pocono. Those are the only ones I know of around here although there probably are more. Oh, and my boyfriend, Jason Hardcastle."

"The Cape Cod cop."

"Yeah, that's the one."

"So, if I ask the ghosts questions, can they hear me?"

"Of course."

"And you'll relay their answers."

"Yes, of course."

"And you won't make up stuff or lie."

"No, I promise I will not. Besides, what's in it for me if I do lie?"

"Nothing, so I guess I'll have to trust you."

Liz stared at the sofa directly at Pete. "Am I looking at Mrs. Capobianco?" she asked.

"No, you're looking at Pete. Lauren's on the other side of Bambi."

"Oh, sorry." She turned her head to focus on the spot where Lauren was sitting. "Mrs. Capobianco, do you mind that your son's here in the room?"

"Have her call me Lauren. Mrs. Capobianco is such a mouthful. Tell her Johnny's really too young to understand what's going on, but if she wants me to have him go into the bedroom, I will."

I relayed the message, and Liz said she'd let it up to Lauren.

"Mrs. Capo… Okay, Lauren, I know your family was notified as soon as we identified your body, so is that why they're here?"

"Yes, they want to arrange for our remains to be transported to Philly for burial. However, they're still waiting for the police to release them." In each case I relayed the reply to Liz.

"Do you know that your father's, er, bodyguards are armed?"

"Yes, I do. They always are, but I believe that's not illegal."

"No, it's not." Liz looked at me and asked, "Three-Zee, what the heck does that body in the cabin have to do with all of this?"

"Liz, here's the problem. We're pretty sure the body in the cabin belongs to the man who carjacked Lauren and Johnny. However, she hasn't seen it yet, so I think she'd have to in order to make a positive ID."

"How the heck can I swing this? I don't think we have anything in our procedures to have a ghost make an ID."

"No, I understand, but is there any way you can get Lauren in to see the body?"

"I don't know. It'll be locked up in the morgue, and I don't necessarily have access."

"That's okay. If you can drive Lauren to the building the morgue is in, probably with Pete along to help, and then give them directions to where in the building the morgue is located, they can go inside and look."

"But there are several locked doors. How the heck would they get in?"

"Liz, ghosts walk through walls and locked doors."

"Oh yeah, so I've been told, but can they ride in cars?"

"Yes, they can."

"Okay, but this is so weird."

"Tell me about it. I have to live with this all the time."

"You do realize that even if Lauren identifies the body, there's not a damned thing I can do about getting him convicted of anything."

"Who cares? If he's the kidnapper, he's dead, and for Lauren, that's all that matters."

"We still will have to find out who shot him."

"Yeah, I know. If his ghost shows up, he might know, but usually ghosts don't remember what happened in the few minutes on each side of when they died. Still, we might get lucky."

I looked at Pete. "Pete, will this work for you?"

"Yeah, we'll go with her now, and she can drop us off at the morgue. She can tell us how to find the place inside the building while we're riding with her." Lauren nodded in agreement, and I relayed this suggestion to Liz.

"But what if the body is in the drawer?" she asked. "Can they open it to look?"

"No, they can't actually open things," I replied, "and it'll probably be totally dark inside the drawer, so even if they walk into it, they can't see in absolute darkness."

"We can wait as long as it takes until they open the drawer," Pete said. Again, I relayed. It would be helpful if there were some sort of ghost translation machine for people who couldn't hear them, but I didn't expect anything like that in the near future, like maybe never. Of course, nobody forecast smart phones or intelligent color-changing light bulbs, either.

"Mm, okay, I can swing by the morgue on the way home."

Pete leaned forward so he could look past Liz at Lauren. "Okay, babe, we've got ourselves a ride."

Bambi asked with a hurt look on her face, "Pete, are you messing around right in front of me?"

"Of course not. Believe me, if I were messing around on you, which by the way I'm not, it would not be in front of your pretty face."

"Oh, then that's all right, I guess," she said.

I looked at Bambi, who was quietly smiling. I'll never understand her.

A Stable Meeting

After my usual crazy morning dealing with hikers, a complaining life-guard, and Cathy coming up with a couple of off-the-wall suggestions, I decided to walk to the new stables during my lunch break. I knew Lizzie was off somewhere checking out horses, but I always have found the company of the animals quite soothing. I popped into the kitchen, begged a couple of carrots from one of the cooks, and headed off.

"I wonder who took it upon himself, or herself for that matter, to eliminate that carjacker, whatever his name was," I said as I patted Honey's nose, which she had poked over the stall door to grab her carrot. Of course, she didn't answer but merely nickered softly.

I turned to Spike, who had poked his nose over his door, probably annoyed because I hadn't fed him first. "Do you have any ideas?"

"No, of course not." Okay, he didn't actually say that, but he did whinny, probably meaning those words. I walked over to him and thanked him for his comment by offering a carrot, which he accepted gratefully.

"Hello in there?" This was spoken, so I spun around, pretty certain the greeting hadn't come from Honey. She had turned her head to look out the big barn door, which I had open because it was a warm day.

"Who?"

A very tall, very big man with dark hair and swarthy complexion walked in front of the opening. "I'm John Capobianco. I'm one of your guests in 505. Are these horses for riding?"

"They will be, Mr. Capobianco, but we haven't opened the stables to the guests yet. Our wrangler is out looking at additional animals today."

"Oh, I was kind of hoping. I do like to ride." I looked at him and decided if we had to provide horses for people with his build, we'd have to invest in a couple of Clydesdales or Belgians.

"No, sir, not yet. We're still working out the logistics."

"So, are you a wrangler, too?"

"No, I'm the Assistant Activities Director. My name is Zelanie Zook. Is there something else I can do for you?"

"No, I guess not. Wait a minute. Zook? Are you the one who found my wife's body?"

"Wife's body?" I knew exactly who he was and to whose body he was referring, but I decided playing dumb was probably the best option for the moment.

"Yeah, my wife Lauren."

"Lauren? I'm not sure I know any Lauren, what did you say, Capobianco?"

"Yes, the body in the wrecked car at the base of your dam. Hers and my son's."

"Oh, yes, of course. I'm so terribly sorry, but I never heard their names." Of course I had, but again, playing dumb. I did notice that Big John, which apparently was his rather appropriate mob nickname according to his late wife, didn't seem all that torn up about the deaths. If my spouse and only child, especially a three-year-old like Johnny, had just been killed, possibly burnt to death, in an auto accident, I'd have been devastated. One could only hope they'd died of smoke inhalation before being incinerated.

"Do you have any idea what happened?" he asked.

"No, not at all. That's a tricky road with all those curves and hills, especially at night, so it's possible your wife merely lost control. It's a very steep embankment. Also, I remember that it had rained earlier that night, so it's possible she skidded on a wet spot."

"I guess that's possible. My father-in-law, her father, is very broken up, too. He's staying in 506." *Broken up, too.* If this behavior signifies "broken up" among mobsters, they have little compassion even for their own. Although I'd seen Papa Guido in various places around the resort during the past few days, he'd never looked broken up to me. Neither he nor his son-in-law had taken any of my hikes or attended any of the Bingo games, not that I'd expected them to, but I had noticed both of them sitting at a table in the lounge last night with their goons at a neighboring table that more or less separated them from any others. I hadn't noticed what they were drinking, and they were certainly too far away for me to overhear their conversations, but then Lizzie had deliberately chosen our table for similar isolation.

"Are you planning to stay here long?" I asked. A perfectly reasonable question from a staff member.

"Yes… No… I really don't know. I guess we're waiting for them to release the bodies."

"May I ask where you live?"

"Philadelphia. My father-in-law is in business there, and I work for him. Anyway, as soon as we can arrange for transport, we'll be on our way." I guess it must be difficult for a mobster to share exactly what kind of "business" he's in. I mean, you certainly couldn't say, "My father-in-law's a Mafia don, and I'm his chief hit man," could you? At least you couldn't say it outside the mob environment where it might be understood and accepted.

"Well, again, I'm so sorry this is the reason you had to come to visit our resort. I hope all goes well with your funeral arrangements."

Big John nodded, turned, and headed outside. I turned and patted Honey's nose. Then I remembered something I probably should have mentioned to Liz last evening. Just before I'd hiked into the woods to make the plaster casts of the footprints, which probably were no longer of any value, I'd noticed one of the goons down in the valley examining the spot where the car had been found. Was that of any value? I had absolutely no idea.

** ** **

I made it back to my office in time to get ready to conduct an afternoon Bingo game. On my way I pondered who might have murdered the carjacker. While it was possible Papa Guido had had him executed, I couldn't imagine how he could have been associated with much of anything. If I hadn't been talking with Lauren's ghost, I would never have paid the least bit of attention to those tracks. After all, people hike on those trails all the time, and I hadn't noticed any evidence that could link Lauren's and Johnny's deaths to anything other than a tragic accident. Liz hadn't mentioned anything, either, but cops do not share information except when it's absolutely necessary, and it was possible she had become disconnected from the investigation of the accident, if such an investigation was even ongoing.

The Bingo game went well, but I was surprised when I came out of the auditorium to see that the sky had clouded over. I checked my phone for the latest weather forecast, and it said showers were predicted. However, it was late April, and April is notorious for showers, so I guessed I couldn't complain, especially since we'd just had a mostly very pleasant run of weather. Besides, rain was necessary at this time of year to, as Bambi would explain, replenish the groundwater. Otherwise, we'd be entering the hot season with a deficit that could lead to a lot of dry vegetation and the risk of fires, which could be devastating.

I've learned to keep an umbrella in my office, now that I have an office, so I headed there to retrieve it. Lizzie was sitting at the desk.

"Any luck finding new horses?" I asked.

"Three more coming next week. There are a couple more that look good, but I'm still negotiating the price. I do have a budget, you know."

"Of course. We all do. Did you hear any more about when your office and living quarters will be ready?"

"The contractor came by this morning just before I left, and he said he was waiting for some materials that should arrive by the beginning of next week. After that, he said it'll take maybe another four or five days, and then I can move in. Will that be okay?"

                                          John A. Miller, Jr.

"Definitely. I know I call this my office, but actually it's merely a place to hang my hat and store my umbrella."

"Hang your hat? I've never seen you wear a hat."

"It's an expression, Lizzie."

Lizzie grinned. "I know. I was just pulling your chain."

"Oh, I guess I should tell you that Big John was hanging around the stable right around lunchtime."

"Big John, as in Lauren's husband?"

"Yeah. He made an excuse that he was checking to see whether we were offering horseback riding yet, but I'm not sure that was his real reason. He apparently didn't know who I was, though, until I mentioned my name. Then he asked me a few questions about the wreck, and I told him I'd never heard his wife's name until now."

"You'll probably go to Hell for lying."

"Probably, but I think I've been destined for that place long before now."

"Haven't we all?"

"He did say they'd probably be here for at least a couple more days. Apparently, they're waiting for the police to release the bodies so they can arrange to have them transported to Philly for burial or whatever."

"Seems odd. Why would people of that self-importance hang around to do something that they'd normally let their minions take care of?"

"Good point. I have no idea."

"Do you think they have other motives?"

"I don't know, but I did wonder whether they had anything to do with that guy's murder in the cabin."

"Why would they? There didn't seem to be anything connecting him to the accident, certainly not to me. I mean, you've been talking to Lauren's ghost, but unless they're like you and can see ghosts, too, they'd have no idea. I doubt the cops know, either."

"Well, that's not exactly true. I spoke with Liz Heyer last evening—she's my state cop friend—and I told her the whole story."

"And did she believe you?"

"I think so. Anyway, I sent Pete and Lauren with her to make sure the body in the morgue's the guy who kidnapped Lauren and Johnny."

"But she can't see them."

"No, she's in the same boat as you are."

"Still, Bambi managed to develop a relationship with a ghost even though she couldn't see or hear him."

"There was that chill."

"I think I'm going to stash a bottle in my drawer. Hanging around with you guys could turn me into an alcoholic yet."

Annoyance Squared

I took my umbrella and headed for the cottage. I went inside, but nobody was there. I knew Bambi was working the dinner shift, so she'd be rather late coming home. Also, Pete and Lauren probably either hadn't been able to view the body yet, or they were on their long walk back, or they had decided to remain invisible. Johnny wasn't around, but maybe he was over at the lodge visiting his father and grandfather, for what it was worth, or maybe he was invisible, too. Ghosts can sometimes be very annoying. Snickers was lying on the sofa taking one of his many daily siestas, but I guess he doesn't count as a person.

I decided to take a short walk, but because of the shower forecast, I decided to leave Snickers in his nice, dry cottage. I'm sure there are cats that don't mind being rained on. Snickers is not one of them. I could carry and use an umbrella, but cat umbrellas probably don't exist.

I walked down to where the maintenance crew had been getting the floating dock ready to put into the lake. They always waited until the risk of freezing had ended because ice might damage the pontoons or decking. If all went well, we'd have rowboats on the lake in a few more days and kayaks and canoes would be available to rent. I knew the crew was waiting for supplies to construct the fixed dock on the pond to replace the one that had collapsed last fall.

Next to the lakeside beach, there's a big grove of trees with picnic tables scattered underneath, tables that had just been placed for the summer. I had just walked into that grove when I heard somebody walking on the dead leaves behind me. I spun around to see a man approaching. When he got closer, I realized it was one of Papa Guido's security team. He looked like the guy I'd seen nosing around the creek yesterday morning.

"Hello, can I help you?" I asked.

"Hey, babe, yeah, maybe you can."

I've never liked being called "babe." I'm not into the whole politically correct thing, but I'm also not an advocate of making women feel inferior. "Babe" to me is just a demeaning term. However, the man was a paying guest, and as an employee of a place like Mountain Woods, one must often bite the bullet and accept the less than perfect.

"I'm not Babe. My name's Zelanie."

"Hey, sorry. Do you work here, cutie?" Okay, "cutie" is even worse than "babe."

"I'm sorry, too, but I'm not your cutie. However, I do work here." Even though some people might consider "cutie" to be a compliment and I'd accept it as such from somebody like Jason with whom I have a relationship, perfect strangers should not be using the term. Besides, this guy didn't look the least bit perfect.

"Oh, I haven't seen you around. Like do you wait on tables in the bar or something when I wish I was there?"

"No, I do not wait on tables although I sometimes act as hostess for dinner seatings. However, I haven't done that since you've been staying here."

"So, what do you do? I mean, a good-looking babe like you could, well, I guess this place doesn't provide that kind of service."

"No, it does *not* provide that kind of service, nor would that be my line of work if it did." There always are rumors about some hotels and resorts that they provide escort services—okay, hookers on call—but Mountain Woods was squeaky clean in that respect, at least as far as I knew.

"Okay, sorry again."

"If that's all you want with me…"

"Well, no, I guess I wanted to ask you whether you'd seen my boss anywhere around."

"Your boss, Mr.…"

"I guess I did forget to tell you my name. I'm Tony, Tony Romano."

"And your boss is…"

"Oh yeah, Mr. Corsana. He's in 506."

"No, I'm afraid I haven't seen Mr. Corsana this evening. I did meet his son-in-law, Mr. Capobianco, this morning, but I don't recall seeing Mr. Corsana anytime today. However, as Assistant Activities Director, I don't necessarily come into contact with all the guests."

"Hey, you can come into contact with me anytime." Tony grinned, a leer that would make the Cheshire Cat vomit.

"Thank you, but I'd rather not. Now, if you'll excuse me…"

"Yeah, okay, I can take a hint," he muttered. The loveable Tony turned and headed back toward the lodge, leaving me in peace standing next to the beach. At least I thought I was in peace. Then I noticed another person headed my way.

Usually prior to opening the beach for swimming and the dock for boat rentals, this area is extremely devoid of people in the evenings, except maybe for those like me trying to get away from the hustle and bustle of the main lodge. Consequently, I was surprised, no make that annoyed, by the arrival of still another person, especially as the previous one had been the picture postcard image of obnoxious. However, as soon as I realized who the newcomer was, I'd have to put him into the same category.

"Good evening, Mr. Pendergast," I said, always the polite employee. Besides, this guy probably could fire me on a whim.

"Yeah, whatever. Have you seen that creep, Corsana?" The man's sharp, grating voice tore at my eardrums.

"No, I have not. In fact, one of his employees was just here looking for him."

"That son of a bitch has been hanging around here doing nothing for too damned long. I'd kick him out of his suite, but George won't let me."

You've heard the term, "between a rock and a hard place." That's exactly where I felt that I was at the moment. I guess I could have agreed with Marvelous Marvin just to get him off my back, but I really agreed with George. After all, a paying guest is preferable to a non-paying one, especially a curmudgeonly part-owner like Marvin, and Papa Guido had really done nothing wrong, at least not in my eyes, except maybe for letting his bodyguards run around with exposed handguns. However, the latter wasn't actually illegal as long as they didn't try to use them.

"Er, were you referring to Mr. Corsana or Mr. Romano?"

"Who the hell is Romano?"

"One of Mr. Corsana's bodyguards, or so I believe."

"Why the hell would I give a horse's butt about a bodyguard? As far as I'm concerned, that whole crew should get out of here."

"I believe Mr. Corsana, his son-in-law, and their associates are here because of the death of Mr. Corsana's daughter."

"Oh yeah, the crispy critter they found down at the base of the dam polluting the creek." Just when I thought a person could go no lower, Marvin took a dive. "So, why doesn't he just grab the ashes and go home?"

"I believe they're waiting for the police to release the bodies."

"Bodies? Oh yeah, the kid, too. Sad, that, but at least he won't grow up to be another hit man like his old man." Marvin didn't look the least bit sad.

"Er, Mr. Pendergast, I'm getting rather cold, so if you don't mind…"

"Yeah, yeah, get outta here. You ain't no use, anyway."

I turned and headed back toward the cottage, hoping that Marvin wouldn't follow me and find out where I lived, although if he'd wanted, I suppose he could have checked the employee housing records. As I walked, I kept looking around hoping that Tony wasn't hanging around for a similar reason, but unless he'd climbed a tree or something, he wasn't anywhere in the area. Anyway, I made it home unscathed.

Bambi came in a few minutes later, looking totally exhausted. "That Papa Guido and his crew are a pain."

"What do you mean?"

"Well, they refuse to come down to the dining room to eat, insisting upon room service for all their meals."

"That's not so unusual. We've had a number of bridal parties and celebrities who want to remain private and get room service. They pay a premium, but so what?"

"Yeah, but the old man keeps complaining the food isn't hot enough or it disagrees with his digestion or whatever, yet we follow his explicit directions as carefully as we can."

"I guess there's no satisfying some people," I said.

"Well, I just hope none of his goons comes down to the kitchen and starts shooting up the place just to make a point. Those guns they carry scare the hell out of me."

"Yeah, they're legal, but I don't like being around people who carry like that. You hope they know what they're doing, but do they?"

"So, how was your day? I haven't seen you since this morning."

I filled her in on my less-than-enjoyable meetings with Big John, Slimy Tony, and Marvelous Marvin.

"Some people have all the luck," she said with a grin. "Any word from Pete or Lauren?"

"No, nothing yet, and Liz hasn't called me with any news, either. Of course, even if the ghosts managed to see the body, they'd have no way of communicating with her until they got back here to one of us."

"Unless one of the people at the morgue can see ghosts."

"Yeah, unless that. Can you imagine how annoying that would be, having to deal with the ghost of somebody while you're carving them up to perform an autopsy?"

"In a way, that's funny."

"Yeah, I guess, or at least to us. To them maybe not so much."

Cabin in the Woods

Bambi and I aren't early to bed and early to rise people, especially on evenings when Bambi doesn't have to get up early the next morning to work the breakfast shift, so at eleven we were still sitting in our living room with the TV playing some mindless show, which was mostly commercials. Anyway, it was then that Pete and Lauren walked through the front door.

"Hey, so how did it go at the morgue?" I asked.

"Okay, I guess," Pete said.

"Yeah, it was him; no question," Lauren said.

"But up until now you haven't been able to tell anybody, right?" I said.

"Right," Pete said. "Apparently, nobody at the morgue or anywhere else around there could see us, and we had to wait until this afternoon for them to get the body out of the chiller to work on it."

"So, Liz doesn't know, yet."

"No. We're expecting you to tell her."

"Yes, I guess that is my job. Bam, you may have to back me up."

"Three-Zee, it won't matter. There's no way anybody is going to be able to use this information for legal purposes."

"No, you're right, but it'll at least give Liz some clues to help steer the investigation into the guy's murder, not that killing him was necessarily a bad thing," I agreed.

"It's a mean thing to say, but I'm kind of glad he's dead," Lauren said.

"Yes, Lauren, I'm sure you feel that way, and I don't blame you."

"By the way, have you seen Johnny?" she asked.

"Not lately. I assume he's either keeping himself invisible for some reason, maybe taking a nap or whatever ghost kids do, or he's over in the lodge with you husband or father."

"Probably the latter," Pete said. "He's definitely not hanging around here or we'd be able to see him. Besides, ghosts don't need to take naps."

"Maybe little ghosts do."

"Okay, but I doubt it."

"Do you think I can wait until morning to call Liz with this information?" I asked. "She won't be too happy if I call her at this hour."

"Yeah, whatever," Pete said. "I have all night. Heck, I guess I have all eternity." He looked at Lauren. "Come on, let's go look for your kid."

** ** **

Because Bambi didn't have to be in the kitchen until eleven, I was the first one up in the morning. I try to be in my office no later than nine because my morning hikes seldom start before nine-thirty or ten. This morning I was out of the cottage a little before eight because I wanted to swing by the stable early to try to catch Lizzie before she went off horse hunting. Among other things, I wanted to fill her in on what Lauren and Pete had discovered now that we'd told her about our ghost-sighting abilities.

"Lauren says it's definitely the guy," I said. "I wonder who he is or was."

"The cops should be able to ID him."

"Yeah, I think they should. He sounds like the kind of guy who would have been on their radar. I called Liz's cell phone to fill her in, but the call went to voice mail. Wait, let me try again." I pressed Liz's number but got the same result. I had left a message after my earlier attempt, so I didn't bother this time.

"Maybe she's on the phone."

"Yeah, or in a dead zone like out at the cabin."

"Did you ever give her those plaster casts you said you made of the footprints?"

"No, but I did save them just in case. Come to think of it, I never told her about seeing one of Papa Guido's goons nosing around the crash site the morning I went out to make the casts."

Does that matter? I mean, it makes sense that he'd want to know as much as possible about how his daughter died."

"Slimy Tony."

"Slimy who?"

"Tony Romano. He's one of Papa Guido's bodyguards, the one I saw down by the creek. He sort of cornered me down by the beach last evening, but I think he was merely looking for some free sex."

"You got away, I hope."

"Yeah, I told him I wasn't interested, so he went away with his tail between his legs." Lizzie gave me a strange look, and then we both broke up laughing.

"I have an idea."

"What?"

"Let's take a ride out to the cabin. If the cops are there, we can merely say we were exercising the horses and didn't know the area was still off limits."

"Is it still off limits?"

"Darned if I know."

"Okay, but I think I have a hike this morning."

"After that, then. My horse viewing appointment for this morning was postponed until tomorrow, so I'm free today."

** ** **

As it turned out, I didn't have a hike to lead. Only one person had signed up, and when she showed up, she decided she didn't want to hike alone—okay, I would have been with her, too, but you get the idea—so I was back at the stable at nine-forty-five to help Lizzie saddle the horses.

The sky was cloudy, but the air was fairly warm. I'd checked the forecast, which did not call for rain. However, when you're dealing with guys who get paid even if they're wrong, you learn to take those forecasts with a grain, no, make that a ton, of salt.

It was actually a rather pleasant morning for a ride, not too hot, not too cold, no wind to speak of, no blinding sun, and the horses seemed to be in good fettle, too. We took our time, no reason not to, but eventually made it along the trails to the cabin. As we approached, I could see several vehicles parked outside including two gray SUVs with the word "Trooper" painted on the sides. I'm not too thrilled with that marking—it can be hard to make out—but maybe that's the idea—make the vehicle not too obviously a police car. Of course, that light bar across the roof is a bit of a giveaway.

We rode up to the cabin—no "POLICE LINE, DO NOT CROSS" tape blocking our way. Spike whinnied just as we started to dismount, so Liz came walking out of the cabin.

"Hey, I didn't expect to see you here," I said. "I've been trying to call you, but the calls went to voice mail."

"Yeah, no signal here. Any news?"

I looked around, hoping her partner wasn't within earshot.

"It's okay," she said. "He's in there arguing with one of the forensics guys, so he won't hear us."

"Lauren says it's definitely the guy. Have you ID'd him yet?"

"Yeah, he's Tyrone Geiger. He's in the files although this is the first time he's worked this area. Actually, he was out on bail from an attempted carjacking out in State College."

"Well, he won't be doing that again, and this'll save them the cost of a trial. I assume you don't have any leads as to who might have saved you all that money."

"No, not yet."

"Oh, although you probably won't need them, I have plaster casts of his footprints that I took back on the trail near the road that passes our dam. I have a couple of his blood samples, too, from where he bled in the grass along the trail. I'm not sure what good they'll be, though, since he's already dead."

"Not much, I guess, but I can take them off your hands with a written statement if you want. We often collect a lot of evidence that turns out to be of little or no use, but it's better to have too much rather than too little."

"Oh, and I saw one of Guido Corsana's bodyguards snooping around down by the creek the same day I made the casts."

"Where the crashed car was found?"

"Yeah, there."

"Unfortunately, it's more or less a public place, and he was probably just snooping around to try to find out any information about the crash. I guess you could file a trespassing claim if you want."

"No, he's a resort guest, so he had a right to be there. Besides, most of that embankment isn't even our property."

I had noticed when Bambi and I had first seen the cabin that it looked to be in excellent condition, almost luxurious for what probably was a hunter's cabin. Of course, some of these cabins are private homes for at least part of the year. "This looks like a pretty nice place," I said. "I wonder who it belongs to."

"We're still trying to check that out in order to notify the owner. Also, we want to make sure Geiger wasn't coming here deliberately. It's possible he was here with the permission of the owner. Of course, he may merely have blundered onto the place and came inside for shelter."

"He was limping on his way here from the wreck."

"Yeah, he had a bad injury to his leg. It had been bleeding, but not enough to be fatal. Still, it would have made walking any distance quite painful."

"So, you'd think the owner's name would be on the property records. Isn't there some sort of tax assessment record?"

"There is, and the taxes are up to date, but the owner is listed as P-Enterprises with a New York City address."

"That's no help."

"No, but it's legal. We're trying to get the name of the principal, but that can take a bit of time because of it being out of state."

Liz looked at Lizzie. "Er, I don't think I've met you before."

"Oh yeah, my bad," I said. "Liz, meet Lizzie. Lizzie, meet Liz." Both women shook their heads and then started laughing. Then they shared their full names.

"Lizzie Borden?" Liz Heyer said. "You're kidding."

"No, it's for real. My parents, I think, have a rather sick sense of humor."

Liz grinned. "Well, it's a good thing the guy inside was shot and didn't have his head cleaved with an axe. Otherwise, I'd have to hold you for questioning."

I pondered for a moment. "I wonder why he did the carjacking the way he did."

"What do you mean?" Liz asked.

"Most carjackers, or at least the ones I hear about on the news, seem to kick the driver out of the vehicle and then drive it away themselves. This one got into the passenger side and had the driver act as his chauffer."

"Maybe he saw the kid in the back, needed a ride, and was planning to let the driver and kid go when he got where he was going."

"But wouldn't he worry that the driver could then ID him."

"Yeah, you're right, but at least then he would get to his destination and not have to dispose of the car nearby, which could be an even bigger giveaway. Maybe he expected to get a ride from his destination to somewhere else, so it wouldn't matter if Lauren knew where she'd dropped him off."

"Or maybe he planned to shoot both her and Johnny, or maybe just her, and ditch the car with them in it."

"Another possibility is that he knew who he was kidnapping, and he wanted to hold the kid, or even both of them, for ransom."

"Too many questions; not enough answers."

"Welcome to the world of police investigations."

Meet the Grinch

Dr. Seuss' immortal character, the Grinch, is generally considered to be a work of fiction, but it seemed we had our own embodiment, perhaps not green, but equally mean-spirited. Also, our version didn't seem to have any heart at all, let alone one that could grow three sizes and make him a nicer guy.

I was sitting in Cathy's office Thursday afternoon working on plans to utilize the woods and clearings more fully around the pond where the new trailer was to be situated. We'd already considered a mid-summer picnic with lights strung between the trees as well as made some early plans for a Halloween Haunted Woods event, similar to the one we'd done last year, but with some more permanent fixtures. The high school ghouls had worked out well, so we planned again to use a crew from there. However, this year we hoped desperately that nobody would die or even be seriously injured.

We had just finished making a list of supplies we'd need for a picnic when the door into the hall burst open and Marvelous Marvin stormed in.

"May I ask what you're doing?" he snapped.

"I beg your pardon, Mr. Pendergast," Cathy said. "We're planning some activities for this summer and fall."

"Well, why does it take two of you? One should be able to make plans, while the other one does some actual work."

"Miss Zook, Zelanie, is my assistant. It's always better to have two heads for something like this, especially if one of us isn't available for the event as happened last year."

"Yeah, you seemed to have a good excuse for not being here for that silly Haunted Woods thing."

"Er, my mother was very ill. Fortunately, she survived her heart attack, but I had to go to Illinois to take care of her for a couple of months."

"And we probably had you on the payroll the whole time while you were off partying."

"No sir, I took an unpaid leave of absence, although Mr. Wylie did offer to pay me during that time."

"I'll have to talk to George about that, throwing away my money on people who don't work. Anyway, I hope you aren't planning to waste money on that damned Haunted Woods crap again. We had to pay all those high school kids and buy all those costumes, and for what?"

"Well, we did make a small amount of profit, and that was good considering how quickly Three-Zee had to throw it together."

"Three-Zee?"

"Er, that's Miss Zook's nickname."

He glared at me. "Yeah, you're the one I saw down at the lake. Silly damned name," he muttered.

I decided to put in my two cents worth, probably a stupid idea, but I never know when to keep my mouth shut. "I'm sorry, sir, but I had no control over how my parents named me or what my friends choose to call me. Anyway, I think the Haunted Woods was a success. It brought people from neighboring resorts to see some of our facilities, which to me smacks of good publicity. Admittedly, we did have those unfortunate events, but even that brought us some free publicity, and it certainly didn't hurt our attendance."

"Ghouls, all of them," he grumbled. Unfortunately, I couldn't exactly disagree with him because at the time I'd thought the same, so I said nothing.

"Did you have a particular reason for stopping in to see us, sir?" Cathy asked.

"Do I need a reason? I just want to make sure my money is being spent properly, and with two highly paid people sitting in here doing nothing, I guess it's not." Marvin turned on his heel, went through the open doorway into the hall, and slammed the door behind him.

Cathy looked at me. "Well, that was fun."

"Yeah, Mr. Nice Guy all the way. He's probably still teed off that Papa Guido commandeered his suite. Anyway, he was last night."

"Last night?"

"Yeah, I was down at the beach when he came wandering by, complaining to high heaven about the Mafia taking over his resort. Well, he didn't actually say Mafia, but he did say he wishes Corsana and his entourage would take their ashes and go home."

"Take their ashes? I assume he was referring to Mr. Corsana's daughter and grandson, but I didn't realize they'd already been cremated."

"They haven't, or at least no more than they already were by the fire in their vehicle, but Marvin actually referred to them as crispy critters."

"How low can you go?"

"I'm not sure, but that comment puts him somewhere below whale poop in my opinion."

"I'm with you there, except I'd use a stronger word than poop."

We went back to our planning, and then George burst into the room.

"That SOB just went up to five and tried to throw Corsana out of his suite."

"And he's still alive to tell about it?" I asked.

"Well, he didn't come down and tell me, so I'm not certain, but one of the maids was up there at the time and overheard the whole brouhaha. I guess Marvin called Corsana a few unprintable names and told him to take what's left of his family and get the hell out of here. The maid reported it to Nattie"—Natalie Calabria is our housekeeping supervisor, a tough cookie in her own right—"and she called me right away. I guess according to the maid, one of Papa Guido's goons then confronted Marvin and threatened him with a gun, so Marvin left the floor, to where I don't know. Now I must go up to five and apologize to Mr. Corsana. Then I must find Marvin and chew him out, which will go over like the proverbial lead balloon. At least he can't fire me because the rest of the board will back me up."

"Just another day in paradise," I said.

"Three-Zee, go to hell."

"Yes sir, boss."

** ** **

Lizzie, Bambi, and I met in the lounge at around nine. The resort has no problem with off-duty employees patronizing the lounge as long as they are dressed appropriately, business casual or better. Of course, Mountain Woods doesn't spring for our beverages. I doubt any employer anywhere does that, although I did hear that at one time brewery workers got to enjoy free beer at lunch or after work. However, I don't know whether that still applies.

"Did he really say that?" Lizzie said after taking a sip of her gin and tonic. At least she wasn't chugging straight whiskey tonight.

"Yes, unfortunately he did. He could set some sort of record for rottenness," I said.

"Probably not. I've met people equally nasty. Fortunately, they're few and far between."

"Has he been harassing you at the stables?" Bambi asked.

"Not really. He's wandered by a couple of times since that first time when I didn't know who he was, but I think he's afraid of the horses. Honey whinnied rather loudly yesterday when he came in, and he immediately looked panicked and ran outside. I did hear him muttering something about the whole thing being a waste of his money, but I ignored him."

"Yeah, that seems to be his style," I said.

I had my piña colada raised to take a sip when an unexpected voice startled me and almost made me drop it. Fortunately, I had a good grip on the glass, so I held on. "My three favorite people, although probably not," the voice, a female one, said.

I finished my sip and then carefully placed the nearly empty glass on the table. "Hello, Liz," I said. "Did they actually give you some off-duty time, or are you here to arrest us on some trumped-up charge?"

"No, I'll leave the trumped-up charging to Hank. He's a lot better at it than I am. I went by your cottage, but nobody was there, or at least nobody that would answer the door. I came up here on the off chance you'd be drowning your sorrows, and voila, here you are."

"Well, our sorrows probably aren't worth drowning, but we're trying, anyway. I'm assuming you stopped by our cottage for more than just a social call."

"What's wrong with just a social call? Okay, you're right. I have an interesting bit of news, I think. We've determined that Mr. Geiger was shot before he died from his leg injury, which apparently wasn't bad enough to be fatal. However, that's not really a surprise, I guess. We're still working on the ownership of that cabin, though. It looks like the owning company is a group of hunters who've established a club of sorts. However, we're having a heck of a time getting a list of their names. Our forensics people have determined that the door lock was either picked or opened with a key because it wasn't damaged in any way. Also, your big fat thumb print was on the bottom of the door latch."

"I thought I wiped it."

"You did, but not thoroughly enough. It's amazing how good finger-print technology has become. Anyway, you're in the clear, at least for the moment, because you had the good sense to report finding the body as soon as you got to a place where you could call us. You didn't shoot him, did you?" With that question she looked around at all three of us.

"No, of course not," I replied. "I admit I was concerned that he might have been the carjacker, but I don't run around shooting people without proof."

Bambi, who had been with me, agreed.

"But if you had proof that he was the carjacker, would you have shot him?"

"Probably not, but mostly because I don't own a gun," I said. "I don't believe Bambi does, either." Bambi shook her head.

Liz looked at Lizzie. "How about you?"

"I wasn't with them, and I wasn't carrying my axe. However, if I'd known what he'd done, I might have felt justified in using it."

Liz motioned for one of the servers and ordered a Scotch and water from that worthy. Then she had Lizzie move to one side and scootched into the space on the bench seat beside her.

"Does she know?" Liz asked, motioning toward Lizzie.

"Yeah, or at least we've told her," I said.

"Okay, then, what are your ghost friends telling you?"

"Nothing since yesterday. Lauren definitely ID'd the guy in the cabin as the carjacker, but she still can't remember exactly what happened. I would suspect that the crash really was an accident because it wouldn't have made sense for Geiger to force an accident that could easily have been as fatal for him as it was for Lauren and her little boy."

"Well, we don't know why he was in the area or where he was trying to go. We are pretty certain that he was in the passenger seat and was thrown out when the car went down the embankment. That seat belt was never fastened, or at least it wasn't in the wrecked car. One could conjecture that he was driving, managed to get out of the car, drag Lauren's body into the driver's seat, buckle her seat belt, and then torch the car, but that would make zero sense. For one thing, the injuries on Lauren's body were consistent with being hit by the exploding air bag from the steering wheel, and it looks like she was actually killed by the top of the car being crushed by a rock in the creek and then hitting her head and crushing her skull."

"I think that might be too much information," Bambi said. I couldn't be sure in the dim lighting, but I think she was turning a bit green.

"I understand," Liz said, "but it helps to know that she wasn't alive to burn to death, a terribly painful thing so I'm told."

"How about little Johnny?" I asked.

"The fire apparently started in the engine compartment from a broken fuel line, so there was enough of a carbon monoxide buildup that he was at least unconscious if not already dead by the time the flames reached him and the gas tank exploded."

This time Bambi got up and headed in the general direction of the ladies' room. I really couldn't blame her.

"Do you get special training in grossing people out?" Lizzie asked.

"No, but it comes with the turf, I guess," Liz replied. "It took me a while, but now I can talk about it. Unfortunately, I still sometimes lose my lunch when I have to look at it."

"That's one way to diet," I said.

"Yeah, but not the one I prefer."

The Hiker from Hell

Friday morning was bright, sunny, and comfortable with a forecast high in the mid-sixties. Twelve people had signed up for the hike, a 'Round-the-Lake jaunt, but I hadn't seen the list of names, which is collected by the front desk and handed to me just before the hike. Therefore, I was appalled when, scanning the names, I discovered "Marvin Pendergast." It was too late to call in sick; I was already standing in front of the lodge with half of the hikers already gathered around.

The count had now reached twelve—one of the women's husbands had opted to join us, which was perfectly okay—when Marvin finally wandered out of the building, muttering to himself. Of course, that made him number thirteen, which didn't help matters one bit. However, he was appropriately attired, in fact, much better attired than many of the other guests with heavy hiking boots, sturdy jeans, and a camouflaged jacket. Whatever else he might be, a shabby dresser he was not, but then he probably could afford the best.

The hike was supposed to begin at ten sharp, but I always delayed at least five minutes if everybody on the list hadn't arrived by then because people sometimes have unforeseen delays that aren't always their fault. Marvelous Marvin did not disappoint when he started complaining because we hadn't set out even though he was the one who was late by three minutes. At that point I wished I had, but he probably would have caught up with us anyway.

We took the clockwise direction, the one I used most often although for no particular reason. The only thing I could figure was that prior to the complete 'Round-the-Lake trail being open, we always had to start out in that direction. At least Marvin didn't complain about that although I was a bit surprised he didn't.

As we rounded the end of the first cove, I noticed several fishermen casting their lines into the water where the trail moved a few yards farther away from the lakeshore, giving them room to settle without blocking the path. It was interesting that Marvin seemed to be watching them closely without griping that they were spoiling his view. In fact, he even asked one of the men whether he'd caught anything and then complimented him when he showed his catch. Maybe fishing was Marvin's hobby or at least something of which he approved.

When we reached the top of the dam Marvin walked to the edge of the dam face and looked down toward the creek where the wrecked car had ended up. "Damned drivers think they can just mess up our property," he muttered.

Unwisely, I said, "I'm sure it was an accident. There is, or at least was, a continuous guard rail along the road over there, but it wasn't strong enough to keep the vehicle from crashing down the hill. I guess it all has to do with speed and angle. Anyway, they haven't gotten around to repairing it yet, but I'm sure they will."

"And we're the ones who have to suffer because of an incompetent highway department."

"Well, it was a terrible tragedy, but actually the resort didn't suffer at all, at least not financially, because the car was removed by a police contractor, and I'm sure the driver's insurance will cover the cost."

"Who asked you?" Marvin snapped.

"Nobody, sir." I turned away and joined the others, who were in the process of regrouping to continue our hike.

As we crossed the new bridge over the spillway, I heard Marvin say, "What a waste of money. We never needed this silly bridge. Now we're stuck maintaining it forever, and for what? A few hikers who are happy that they have a remote control when they're at home, so they don't have to get off their fat duffs to change the TV channel." I noticed several of the hikers giving Marvin dirty looks, but I really had nothing I could say to them, at least not when Marvin was in earshot. I also admit to falling into that category of people who don't like to get off my duff, which I strongly maintain is *not* fat, to change the TV channel, but then I've never known a time when our TV did not have a remote control. I understand, though, that back in prehistoric times such TVs did exist. Hey, telephones once had dials, too.

We all made it alive to the end of the pond where a crew was busily erecting the new dock to replace the one that had collapsed in fall. They wanted to have it in place for the opening of boating, which was scheduled for next week. Needless to say, Marvin complained about the cost of that, too. Judging from the looks he was getting from several other hikers, I wasn't about to vouch that he'd make it back to the lodge without somebody throwing him in the lake, although at least for that part of the hike the trail doesn't border the water except briefly along the forest road.

I've had terrible hikes in the past including one where the complainer was actually struck by lightning, probably a genuine act of God, but by the time I reached the lodge and the other hikers abandoned me for their gourmet buffet lunch, I was almost praying that God would invoke a similar punishment for Marvin.

After parking my jacket in my office, I stuck my nose, okay my whole body, into the kitchen where I found Bambi busily breading something that looked like fish. "I'm gonna kill him," I said.

"It's probably not worth spending the rest of your life in jail just to rid the world of a pile of camel dung."

"Heck, I might get a thank you note from the judge."

"Nah, they never seem to see it from your point of view. We can always hope a meteorite falls out of the sky and lands on his head."

"What are the odds of that happening?"

"Lightning or a rattlesnake bite are more likely."

"Or maybe a mountain lion attack. Bam, are there mountain lions in the Poconos?"

"I'm not sure although I guess it's possible. I think there are bobcats, though."

"Still, I wouldn't want the poor cat to eat him and then die. I'm sure he has cyanide running through his veins."

"Without a doubt."

At that moment I heard a commotion from the other end of the kitchen, which is enormous, and I could see Marvin arguing with the head chef. I turned around and beat it out of there. Let Bambi fight her own battles. She could always bean him with a breaded filet.

** ** **

If you think things couldn't get much worse, think again. While I was setting up the auditorium for an afternoon Bingo session, I had my back turned to the audience area where the players would gather at long tables. Consequently, I didn't notice who came in and took seats, not that it mattered because there was no admission charge—no particularly valuable prizes for this afternoon's games—so it was open to all guests.

After I finished arranging the little ping-pong ball gizmo that would push specially marked balls into a slot, which then I could mark on a video display, I turned around and scanned the crowd—okay, about twenty people, mostly older women. Then I saw him, Slimy Tony Romano, sitting in the front row grinning at me. I was surprised because men of Tony's age, probably late thirties, and occupation, probably hit man but at least bodyguard, don't seem to frequent Bingo halls. As it was, he was the only male guest who'd shown up.

I picked up a pile of paper Bingo card packets and markers and started distributing them. When I passed Tony, he said, "Hey, babe, aren't you glad to see me?" I guess it's not within my job description to ignore guests, but I merely handed him his supplies and continued on. If I ignore him, maybe he won't bother me in the future, I thought.

The game progressed normally, and Tony behaved himself. He won a couple of games, but the prizes are simple things like a free soft drink at the lounge or some gift toiletries, so nobody went away wealthier than they'd been when they came in.

Afterward, I was collecting the scrap paper from the tables when Tony approached me. "Mr. Corsana would like to talk to you," he said.

"Did he say why?"

"Not to me. You'll have to find that out for yourself."

"Couldn't he have come down here or to my office?"

"Mr. Corsana does not come to people. People go to Mr. Corsana."

"Ah. Okay, but do you mind waiting until I finish putting my stuff away?"

"No, not at all. He didn't say it was urgent, or I would have made you go upstairs to see him right away."

While I finished cleaning up and Tony hovered over by the entrance, I considered Papa Guido's request. While I guess it was in order—our job is to serve, within reason, of course—I couldn't recall ever being asked by a guest to attend him or her in their room. Room service and housekeeping were the folks who usually did that, although I guess George occasionally had to visit people of importance. I'm not sure whether Guido Corsana would be considered a person of importance, but when his personal support staff wanders around the premises brandishing firearms, that moves him up several notches on the list. Tony wasn't actually brandishing, but I was pretty sure he was packing. Papa Guido was here to collect his daughter's remains, so I decided he wasn't looking for me to assuage some romantic desire on his part. Tony was another thing entirely, but I figured I wouldn't have to visit his room.

We rode the elevator together to five, and then I led the way to 506 at the end of the hall. At least Tony was behaving himself for the time being.

I knocked on the door, which was promptly opened by Tony's counterpart. After all, why have one bodyguard when you can have at least two. "Come in," he said.

The man, almost a twin of Tony Romano in appearance, led the way across the small foyer and into the suite's living room. I'd actually seen little of Papa Guido since he'd arrived because when he was actually in residence, he had mostly remained in his room. I rather expected a Marlon Brando Godfather voice, so I was surprised by a smooth bass without a trace of Italian accent. "Miss Zook, I presume."

"Yes sir, I'm Zelanie Zook."

"Hm, interesting name. I understand you're the person who discovered my daughter's and grandson's bodies."

"Yes sir. Well, I didn't actually discover them because one of the hikers in the group I was leading actually spotted the wrecked car from the top of the dam. However, I'm the person who went down to investigate; actually, me and one of the other hikers."

"Ah, yes, Mr. Jasper. Unfortunately, Mr. Jasper is no longer with us." I guess I must have looked as shocked as I felt because Papa Guido chuckled and continued with, "I see my reputation has preceded me. No, I have not had Mr. Jasper eliminated in the manner you may be thinking. It's merely that he checked out last Sunday—I'd already spoken with him prior to then—and returned home to Newark because he said his vacation had ended and he had to go back to work." Corsana shook his head. "Why anyone would choose to live in Newark is beyond me." As I've mentioned, I don't keep track of most guests' comings and goings, so I hadn't noticed DJ's departure. Bambi might had known because of helping out at the desk on Sundays, but she'd have had no reason to tell me, especially as I didn't recall ever mentioning his name to her.

"So, what can I do for you?" I asked, not having the foggiest idea.

"I'd like you to accompany Mr. Romano to perform a more thorough examination of the crash site. Because you saw it firsthand, you will be able to show him exactly where the car landed."

The request was reasonable, I guess, but I was less than elated by the thought of accompanying Slimy Tony anywhere. Tony had come into the room, so I glanced at him where he was standing off to one side, and the leer on his face said it all. Either Corsana didn't notice, or he didn't care. "Will that be now?" I asked, hoping he'd say something like next year would be fine.

"Yes, of course. I'd like to find out as much as I can about the crash prior to returning home with the remains." Okay, that shot down that hope. I vaguely recalled a Greek myth we'd learned about in high school English class about a woman named Pandora who'd released all the ills of the world from a box of some sort but had slammed shut the lid before letting out hope. It looked like hope was still hiding in that box and not about to help me. I considered trying to postpone the inevitable, but I had nothing on my plate for the remainder of the afternoon, and I supposed he could have gone over my head to Cathy or George and, as a well-paying guest, had my time assigned to him for as long as he needed. There are certain requests that would have definitely been off-limits, but accompanying somebody to a crash site so that person could do a "more thorough investigation" wasn't one of them.

Tony the Tiger

As we walked toward the elevator from Papa Guido's suite, Tony said, "We'll take one of the cars."

"What do you mean? I was assuming we'd walk."

"No, I walked over there last week when I was checking the place out, but I nearly broke my neck trying to go down the face of the dam. Also, if we do find anything, it'll be easier to bring it back in the car."

"I kind of doubt we'll find anything considering that I'm sure the police have been over the area with a fine-tooth comb. Also, you've already checked it out."

"Yeah, but you know where things were. I don't."

"But the cops did. After all, they were the ones who removed the wreck and the bodies, so they knew exactly where everything was."

"Yeah, well, you never know."

We entered the elevator, and I pressed the "L" button for lobby. We were alone in the elevator, so I asked, "Do you have any idea when the bodies will be released?"

"We think today or tomorrow. That's why Guido is so concerned about looking for any more clues before we head back to Philly."

"I'm kind of surprised you haven't all gone back already, or at least he and his son-in-law going and leaving you and the other bodyguard behind."

"It's his call, and he wanted to stay. Anyway, he'll have to call the funeral home to send up the hearses when the bodies are released."

"You could have done that."

"Yeah, well, like I said, it's his call."

** ** **

I always enjoy riding in a true luxury car, which both of Papa Guido's were. Unlike my ancient vehicle or Bambi's equally ancient pickup, the Lincoln had springs that actually sprung and the leather seats were the height of comfort. I wondered what it would be like to ride in the ultimate luxury car, a Rolls Royce, but I suspected I'd never find out unless I married a prince, a rather unlikely thing. I'd have to make do with the Lincoln, at least for now.

So far Tony had behaved himself, paying attention to his driving and not obviously violating any traffic laws. Of course, he probably had been trained in that because a person of Guido Corsana's importance wouldn't want to be held up by any impertinent police officer trying to hand out a ticket. I was sure Papa Guido had friends in high places, but sometimes there's a delay between the event and summoning those friends. In Philly the cops probably knew his vehicles and courteously ignored his drivers' transgressions, but I doubted the police in the Poconos were as well informed.

Anyway, we made it to the crash site unscathed, and Tony actually found a spot big enough to pull the enormous vehicle completely off the road. We were only about a hundred yards past where Lauren's car had crashed through the guardrail, which was still bent and broken. Knowing how quickly highway departments respond to needed repairs, I wasn't holding my breath for this one.

The embankment over which Lauren's car had tumbled is probably as steep as the dam face, but unlike the dam face it's grassy and somewhat easier to navigate. As I stood at the top looking down at the creek, I considered sliding down on my butt, but that would have led to at least two problems. First, it would have completely ruined my best pair of jeans. Grass stains are notoriously hard to remove. Second, Tony would have probably laughed his head off and, worse, shared the information. I didn't really care what Tony thought of me, but depending upon with whom he shared, I could have had to live with it being brought up for quite a while.

As we carefully made our way downward, trying not to fall on our noses or worse, I noticed a couple of large rocks hidden in the tall grass. If I'd hit one of those while sliding… Okay, another good reason not to.

We spent the better part of an hour looking for anything out of the ordinary. However, the only things not native to a creek bed or grassy hillside were a few crumpled cigarette packs, some used tissues, and a broken bolt, which may or may not have come from Lauren's BMW as it rolled down the hill. Tony had pulled a bundle of plastic bags from his pocket and bagged the bolt. I supposed it would be possible to trace the part and determine whether it came from the car, although I didn't know whether it could have come from another crash sometime in the past. I had no real knowledge of the history of the area. Heck, it could even have fallen there while the dam was being built. However, it wasn't rusty, so that spoke for it being a recent addition to the area.

We made our way back to the Lincoln and got in. "Well, that was kind of a waste of time," I said.

"Not necessarily. At least now we know nothing was missed. That broken bolt I guess could have been part of the suspension or steering and caused Lauren to lose control."

"Or, it could have been broken off while the car rolled down the hill and had nothing to do with causing the crash."

"Yeah, that, too."

"Did you know Lauren well?"

"Pretty well. I sometimes had to watch over her or the kid when Big John had to go out of town."

"Mm. Did that happen often?"

"Often enough."

"You don't know why Big John had to go out of town so often, do you?"

"No, and it's no business of yours if I do."

"Right. Sorry. I'm just a bit nosy."

"Don't be, at least not if you want to keep your pretty nose."

I accepted Tony's comment about my nose, which was actually the first thing he'd said about my appearance since just after the Bingo games. So far, except for that brief leer in Papa Guido's suite, he'd avoided any sexist moves or comments. Besides, I've been told by others that my nose is cute, and "pretty" is a synonym for "cute," right?

Tony pulled out of the parking space and continued along the road after I told him I could guide him back to the lodge in this direction. The road is fairly narrow, too narrow to turn around a battleship like the Lincoln, so making some kind of U-turn wasn't really an option.

I almost succumbed to a temptation to tell him about Tyrone Geiger and his carjacking of Lauren and Johnny, but then I realized I had no evidence of that except for what I'd been told by a ghost. Talking about Lauren's and Johnny's ghosts could open up a whole new field of interest for Papa Guido and Big John Capobianco, a field of interest in which I wanted no part.

"Did you like Lauren?" I asked, why, I don't know.

"What are you saying?"

"Sorry, I didn't mean that in a bad way. It's merely, I wondered whether she was a nice person."

"A very nice person. Good-looking, friendly, and kind, unlike her SOB of a husband." Tony stopped talking for a moment. "Forget I said that."

"Yeah, I understand. He doesn't look like the kind of guy you'd want to cross."

"Definitely not. Let's just say I have a pretty good idea why he went out of town so often, but I'm trusting you not to say I said so." That seemed a bit convoluted, but I'm pretty sure I caught his drift.

"I guess it's possible it wasn't an accident."

Tony looked at me. "What do you mean?" Fortunately, he turned his head back to look at the road because he had nearly driven into a large tree just beyond a sharp curve. The car missed it by inches.

"Oh, nothing. Just thinking about all the options. An accident on that road is most likely, especially if a deer came running out of the woods and she swerved or something. After all, I haven't heard anything to the contrary."

"If somebody caused her to have that accident, even an oncoming car in the wrong lane, I'll rip him apart."

"But how would you ever know?" I was intrigued by his sudden passion to exact vengeance for Lauren's death. However, I wasn't about to tell him that the perp had already met a probably suitable end, one of which I'm sure he would approve.

"There are ways." After that he clammed up and said nothing more on our return trip to the resort.

** ** **

"Do you think I should have said something?" I asked the group gathered in our small living room. It was a lot of people, with me, Bambi, and Lizzie sharing the sofa, Pete and Lauren somehow both squeezed onto the easy chair, and Johnny and Snickers playing on the floor.

"I don't think so," Bambi said. "Why open that can of worms?"

"Yeah, I admit I'm working strictly from what you told me because I can't see or hear Lauren, but what Papa Guido and his group don't know probably won't come back to haunt you," Lizzie said.

"Like us," Pete said. I ignored him.

"I wonder whether the police are ready to release the bodies," I said. "Tony seemed to think it'll be within the next couple of days. I haven't seen Liz today to ask her, but I can't imagine they'll keep the bodies on ice any longer than they need to, and Liz had already told me there's no official suspicion of foul play. I guess they had to test for alcohol and drugs, but after those tests there'd be no reason to keep them."

"Wouldn't your suspicions about Tyrone Geiger mean something?" Lauren asked.

"Yes, if at least a couple of people on the police force could see you, but otherwise, not a bit. I know Jason on Cape Cod, who can see ghosts, doesn't bring it up when he's at work because he's the only member of the Chatham Police who can, or at least as far as he knows. I think Liz believes me, but who'd believe her?"

"Good point," Pete said. "However, this being invisible to most people can get annoying at times."

"But it comes in handy when you're checking out the babes in their showers," I said.

Pete grinned. "Yeah, there is that. Even better than Harry Potter's cloak of invisibility."

Bambi laughed. "That's okay. Pete can go out and work up an appetite as much as he wants as long as when it's feeding time he comes home to me."

"Oh, puh-leeze," I groaned.

"Are you planning to accompany your husband and father back to Philly?" Bambi asked Lauren.

"I haven't decided yet. Actually, I've been feeling the urge to move on, and if I do, I'll take Johnny with me."

"Yes, that makes sense," I said. "Now that you've identified the who, how, and probably why associated with your death, you should be able to do that. Unless you're able to meet up with a person in Philly who can see and hear you, you'll just have to wander around incognito there. Of course, you could listen in on your father's and husband's conversations to find out what they're really up to, but do you really want to know?"

"Not really. I pretty much know already. I can do without the grisly details."

"Yeah, I figured as much. The only loser here will be Snickers because he'll be losing a full-time playmate." Snickers looked at me as if he understood and then meowed. Of course, that could merely have been a reaction to something Johnny had done. I'll probably never know.

Departures

After eating lunch on Saturday, I had just returned from the stable, where I had taken some carrots to feed to Honey and Spike, when I noticed the two black Lincoln SUVs pulled up under the front portico of the lodge. Tony and his counterpart were busily loading luggage into the back.

"Hey, Tony, what gives?" I asked after walking over to him. I felt I had established some sort of rapport with him yesterday considering that he'd stopped calling me babe.

"Heading home in a few minutes. The cops released the bodies, and the hearses are on their way. We're not going to try to set up some sort of funeral procession because there are simply too many miles for us to stay together. We'll do that later in Philly after the actual funeral."

"Mm, that makes sense. Well, I hope things go well for you on the drive south."

"Yeah, thanks."

** ** **

A half-hour later I saw Lauren and little Johnny follow Papa Guido and Big John to the cars. Lauren had tears in her eyes, and Johnny waved goodbye as his father and grandfather got into their SUVs and were driven away. I walked over to the two ghosts, made sure that my back was turned to the main entrance so nobody there could see my lips moving, and asked, "How do you feel?"

"I'm surprised I feel so sad," Lauren said. "I guess it comes from not knowing what will happen after I move on. I'm guessing at some point I'll meet up with them, but I suppose that all depends upon the dividing line between Heaven and Hell."

"If there is a Hell."

"Or a Heaven."

"It wouldn't make sense for you to survive as ghosts and then merely fade away after you move on."

"Does any of this make sense?"

"Not a bit. The priests and preachers tell us all sorts of things about the afterlife, but do they really know? I suspect most of them know even less than we do unless, of course, they can see and talk to ghosts, too."

"Have you ever met a ghost who's moved on and come back?"

"No, never. By the way, how's Johnny handling it?" I had noticed that the little boy had wandered over to the lawn that bordered the drive, apparently watching the antics of a couple of squirrels.

"Surprisingly well. I merely told him that we'd see Daddy and Grandpa later. He's used to them not being around us all the time, so that seemed to satisfy him."

"Yeah, that's all you can do."

"It looks like you're all alone here now," a voice said from behind me.

I spun around, hoping my movement didn't raise the curiosity of anybody who might be watching. "Pete, stop sneaking up on me like that. Anyway, she isn't all alone. She has us."

Pete walked past me so I could again turn my back to the lodge. No point is having people watch me standing there apparently talking to myself.

"Not for much longer, I suspect," Pete said.

"No, I think I'm ready. I'll just go collect Johnny and then, well, who knows?"

"Yeah, who knows."

Lauren walked slowly to the lawn where Johnny was running after the squirrels and trying to grab them because they didn't seem to see him. Of course, when he grabbed, his hand went right through them. They jumped, probably startled by the sudden chill, but didn't seem to be spooked.

The little boy looked up at his mother, walked to her side, and then they both faded away. I admit to a few tears in my own eyes. They had been nice ghosts, and I felt bad that they hadn't had more years to enjoy life. I glanced at Pete, and he seemed to have tears in his eyes, too. Maybe he wasn't as callous as he sometimes seemed.

** ** **

I left Pete and made my way back into the main lobby and then crossed it and entered an Employees Only door. The past few minutes had centered around several departures, all but two of whom I'd been pretty happy to see leave. Then I saw over by the service elevator a person I'd have been even happier to see leave. Marvin was berating Natalie, which I thought was interesting because Natalie was notorious for berating her own housekeeping staff. I had turned toward my office to avoid both of them when I heard Marvin call, "Hey, you, come over here!"

I turned, tried my best to look surprised, and said, "Were you talking to me?"

"Yeah, you. Tell this woman I need my room made up right away."

"Er, your room. Didn't housekeeping take care of it this morning?" I glanced at Natalie, who was giving Marvin the evil eye.

"Not that room, Marvin snapped. "My suite."

"I didn't know you were in a suite, Mr. Pendergast. I thought you were in 412, which I don't think is a suite. Of course, you could have moved. I'm afraid I don't keep up with where guests are staying."

"Well, you should. Anyway, this woman should know, and I'm now in 506."

"Oh, did you arrange that through the front desk? I'm sure they'll switch you if it's available."

"It better be," Marvin grumbled. "Terrible way to treat the guy who owns the place. Next thing you know, I'll go home, and my housekeeper will have moved some vagrant off the street into my own bedroom." He turned his back and stomped down the hall toward George's office.

"Sorry about that," I said to Natalie.

"If I kill him, will you testify against me."

"I never saw a thing, but I'll buy you dinner."

"Thanks. I'll hold you to that."

With the number of people lining up to take potshots at Marvelous Marvin, I could see I was going to have a lot of forgetting to do, and those dinners could get expensive.

The Boating Party

For a change Bambi and I both had Monday off, something that happens only every five or six weeks. Although that day usually finds us on the road to Lancaster County to visit our families, our gas money was rather low at the moment and both of us had tires that were showing significant signs of wear, so until we could amass some extra cash, quite a lot of it actually, we were keeping our trips closer to home.

One thing we could do that wouldn't cost us anything was take out one of the rowboats on the lake now that the floating dock and the boats were in the water for the summer. Also, work on the new fixed dock in Abner's Pond near where the new trailer was scheduled to arrive next week was complete, so we could make that an intermediate destination. While I walked by it regularly, I hadn't approached that area by water since early last fall just before we started the Haunted Woods, and then the old dock was way too rickety to use, so this would be an interesting trip.

Some of you may wonder why I'm still calling the pond "Abner's Pond" when it hasn't been owned by Abner Whitelaw for well over a year, and that worthy is residing in a state prison somewhere or other in Pennsylvania and will be for some years to come. I guess it's something we've been calling it ever since Bambi and I started working at Mountain Woods, and the name has stuck. I've never heard it called anything else nor have I ever seen it named anything at all on the topographic maps of the area I've seen, so I guess Abner's Pond is as good a name as any.

We both slept in and made it to breakfast by nine-thirty, just before the employee buffet closed. It's not gourmet, but it's included. Then we wandered down to the boat rental kiosk where Harry Walker was set up to rent rowboats, canoes, and kayaks to guests. He also would take a rowboat that was reserved for his use to row out to the buoys where the other rowboats were tied and covered and then tow a boat back to the dock for the guest to use. In a luxury resort, guests expect that kind of service.

While Bambi and I as employees didn't have to pay to rent a boat as long as one was available, Harry didn't row out to get one for us, either. We'd have to row out and retrieve one ourselves. However, he did hand us a pair of oars for the boat we'd be using.

"Don't bring this one back with bullet holes," he warned with a grin.

"Harry, that happened one time, and it wasn't a bullet hole. It was made by a shotgun pellet. Besides, Abner's no longer a threat."

"Whatever, but I'm the guy who had to patch it."

"Yeah, and I'm the girl who wound up with a leg full of the damned pellets," Bambi complained.

"Hey, if you go looking for trouble…"

"We weren't looking for trouble. We just happened to be in the wrong place at the wrong time."

"Like at midnight in a pond belonging to somebody else with warning signs at the entrance about trespassers being shot."

"Hey, regardless of property rights, I don't think people have the right to shoot you if you happen to stray onto their land."

"Stray, hell. You went there deliberately."

"Yeah, okay, that was years ago."

"Slightly less than two, to be precise."

Harry has been harassing us about the incident where Abner shot at us with a shotgun while we were snooping in his pond at midnight ever since we came back that night, Bambi with a leg full of pellets, and the boat with a hole where one of the pellets missed Bambi. At least now we can laugh about it.

"Give me the damned oars and shove it," Bambi said with a laugh.

"Shove what and where?"

"The oars, and you know where."

"But then they won't do you any good." Harry reached behind him, lifted a pair of oars from their rack, and handed them to me. Then Bambi and I walked to the dock where I used his rowboat to retrieve another from a buoy and tow it back to the dock. Bambi helped me uncover the new boat, and then I got into it and put the oars in their locks while Bambi carried the cover up to the kiosk. Yes, the guests save a lot of time and effort by having Harry retrieve the boat for them.

In the process of retrieving our boat, I had dipped my hand into the water several times. It was still way too cold for swimming, so I hoped we didn't capsize somewhere out there where the water was deep and maybe even colder.

"I'll row first," I said. "You can take care of the return trip."

"I forgot gloves," Bambi said.

"Why do you need gloves? It's not *that* cold."

"I don't want blisters on my hands. It's tricky enough cooking without them."

"You have to wear those plastic gloves anyway, so a leaking blister won't contaminate the food."

"Hey, but it hurts if the blister breaks."

"Wuss," I muttered as I used the oars to push away from the dock. Bambi, meanwhile, had positioned herself in the seat in the stern.

My legs are in good shape from all the hiking I do regularly, but my arm muscles began to ache by the time we'd checked out two of the coves and then started back toward the creek after turning at the warning signs near the dam. When he lived there, Abner had two huge signs bordering his creek that said trespassers would be shot. Those signs had been among the first things removed after the resort bought the property, but I still felt a bit nervous as we rounded the small bluff and entered the creek. I remembered that he'd even shot at me, Mom, and Aunt Gladys while we were still well out in the lake, which even then was completely owned by Mountain Woods. Fortunately, we'd been too far away for the shotgun pellets to hit us.

By the time we reached the new dock my arms were aching like toothaches. Okay, maybe not quite like that, but you get the idea. Bambi crawled past me to grab the bow rope and then climbed out on the dock and tied the rope to one of the cleats that had been installed there just for that purpose. In summer we intended to activate the snack bar in the new trailer, and arrival by boat or other watercraft would be encouraged. However, we had no plans to allow motorized vessels. The lake was simply too small.

As I climbed from the boat onto the dock, I said, "I'm surprised Pete didn't join us."

"Yeah, I am, too. I offered this morning when we left for breakfast, but he said he wasn't interested."

"He's probably up at the indoor pool checking for scantily clad women."

Bambi laughed. "I think that's why he doesn't want to move on. He's afraid that women in Heaven will be fully clad."

"The ones in Heaven probably will be. The ones who aren't fully clad might be in the other place."

We walked across the clearing and around the line of trees that separated the pond from where the trailer was to be placed. All was ready for its arrival, which as I mentioned earlier was scheduled for next week. We were about to turn back toward the dock when I heard a thumping and gasping noise. I looked up toward where the trail from the forest road emerged from the woods and watched a young man running toward us. He was clad in ankle-length black running tights, a black long-sleeved tee shirt, and bright red running shorts and sneakers, probably a guest out for a run. However, when he reached us and stopped, bending over to clasp his ankles and gasping for breath, I got a good look at his face, and he looked somewhat familiar.

"Good afternoon," I said, ever the polite manager. "Er, you look somewhat familiar. Are you a guest here at Mountain Woods?"

The young man, probably in his early twenties, stood up and between gasps he said, "No, I work here, but it's my day off."

"Oh, it's our day off, too. I'm Zelanie Zook, Assistant Activities Manager, and this is Bambi Bamberger. She's a cook and also works sometimes at the front desk.

"Well, I guess I sort of work for you, but I haven't met you yet. I'm Luke Walker. I'm the new lifeguard. I interviewed with Cathy, but you were busy leading a hike at the time."

I'd have to talk to Cathy about that. While she had every right to hire, and fire, for that matter, without consulting me, I'd sort of like to know about new employees. "When did you start?"

"Let's see, last Tuesday."

I thought for a minute. "Yes, I did have a hike around the lake that morning, and then in the afternoon I went over to another trail to do something."

"Are there other good trails around here for running besides this one?"

"You've already been on the forest road, which is great, and there's the trail around the lake. If you follow that lane a little ways—I pointed toward the lane that led out toward the paved road—you'll find a trail that leads off to the left. That will eventually cross a road and continue for quite some distance. The resort property ends just before the road, but I've been as far as a hunter's cabin that's a good mile beyond it, and so far nobody's challenged me." I didn't mention that a person inside the hunter's cabin had sported a bullet hole. There are things you don't tell a new acquaintance at first meeting.

Bambi looked at him. "Do people sometimes call you Luke Sky-walker?"

"All the time. Fortunately, my father's name isn't Anakin Skywalker or Darth Vader. My parents never told me why they named me Luke."

"Well, we just hired a wrangler to run our new stable, and her name is Lizzie Borden," I said.

"Yeah, so?" Okay, maybe the Fall River Legend isn't as well known as I thought. I wondered whether my brother Joe, more of a contempo-rary of this guy, had ever heard of it. Then it dawned on me. Harry's last name was Walker, too.

"You wouldn't happen to be related to Harry Walker, would you?"

"He's my older brother."

"Oh, okay. He's a good guy."

"Yeah, he is, I guess." Younger brothers don't always appreciate their older siblings. Mine certainly doesn't.

Luke took his leave and Bambi and I watched as he headed off along the lane, probably to check out the other trail. Then we headed back to the dock and our rowboat.

"Your turn to row," I said as I stood by the tied rope.

"Okay, but I'd better not get sore arms. I need them in good shape to chop veggies and lift pots."

"Actually, yours are probably in much better shape than mine. I get a lot of leg exercise, but arms not so much."

"Yeah, leg exercise from running away from trouble."

"Bam, shut up and row!"

** ** **

When we got back to the dock, I jumped out, made fast the painter—I know that it's the rope used for tying up the boat, but it always sounds like tying up the guy painting the boat—and waited for Bambi to climb out. Then we walked up the slight grade to drop off the oars at the kiosk where Harry appeared to be counting some fishing lures. Yes, we sell those, too.

"We met your brother," I said.

"Oh, Luke. Yeah, he's my brother."

"You don't sound too enthusiastic."

"We've never been close. He's the athletic one. He likes running, swimming, and shooting."

"Shooting?"

"Yeah, he holds several marksmanship badges."

"Mm, interesting. Well, we left the boat tied to the dock. It's not dirty or full of water, so you can rent it out if anybody wants it."

"What, no bullet holes?"

"Hey, once is enough," Bambi said. "Besides, I got more holes in me than in the boat."

"Yeah, you'll have to get a pair of steel pants. Maybe one of those medieval suits of armor."

"Good idea, but not so great for swimming."

"Not unless you can breathe water."

Black Is the Color

After we returned to the lodge, I made my way to Cathy's office while Bambi wandered off, probably to our cottage. Cathy was in and sitting behind her desk.

"I met our new lifeguard," I said.

"Oh, Luke Walker."

"Yeah, I was kind of surprised because I didn't know you'd hired a new one. I guess you know he's Harry's brother."

"Yes, of course. We check out all references as you well know."

"Cathy, I'm not complaining or anything, but as Assistant Activities Director, exactly who do I have the authority to supervise, without overriding you, of course?"

"Er, I never thought about it because I never had an official assistant before. Hm, I'd say everybody who reports to me, which are the lifeguards, the staff like Harry and Jeff who take care of the boats and outdoor activities, Lizzie Borden, and yourself—no, that makes no sense because I can't envision you giving yourself orders. I'd say the people who help set up the auditorium except they really don't report to me. They're either under maintenance or housekeeping."

"Is there some sort of official chain of command?"

"I don't know. I don't recall ever seeing one. Probably George has something like that."

"It might be helpful, just so we all know where we stand. I admit I've never in my life had any sort of supervisory position before, but it would help if I knew where I could give orders or merely beg for help."

"Yes, I understand. By the way, what did you think of Luke?"

"Okay, I guess. He was out for a run—too much effort for me. Anyway, Harry said he's really into the physical stuff like running and swimming, which I guess is appropriate for a lifeguard. Also, Harry said he's quite a sharpshooter."

"Hm, I don't recall seeing that on his resume, but then it's not something that would mean much here. We don't have a shooting range, nor do we have plans to install one, unless of course George and the board decide otherwise."

"Yeah, there's always that."

"By the way, have you been down to the stables in the past couple of days?"

"Yeah, Saturday morning. I'm trying to stay on the good side of the horses."

"Probably a good idea. Do you think the apartment will soon be ready for Lizzie to move in? The reason I'm asking is because housekeeping wants her space in the employee lodging. I guess they have a new maid coming."

"I'll check with Lizzie. She'll know better than we do when it's adequate. I heard they're having trouble getting the gold-plated plumbing fixtures for the bathroom."

"The what?" Cathy looked shocked.

"Just kidding. Lizzie seems to be the kind of person who'd be happy with a pump handle."

"That's what I thought, although what's on the plans is a lot better than that."

** ** **

When I got back to the cottage, I discovered Bambi and Pete snuggled on the sofa watching TV. I'm not sure exactly how it's possible to snuggle with a ghost, but somehow those two manage.

"Who wants to go for a horseback ride?" I asked.

"Wow! You're really getting into this physical activity stuff," Bambi said. "My arms still ache from rowing."

"Well, now it's time for you to get an ache in your butt, too. Come on. Pete, you can come with us."

"You know I can't sit on a horse. Well, I guess I could, but I can't imagine how I could control the poor beast."

"No, but you can run alongside if we ride slowly enough. You don't get tired or out of breath."

"What breath? Yeah, I can do that." He looked at Bambi. "Come on, dear, let's go." Bambi gave him a dirty look and pushed herself up from the sofa while I grabbed the remote and switched off the TV. I'm never sure whether the word he's using is "dear" or "deer", but I guess in Bambi's case either one would do.

"Well, at least we don't have to deal with that crew from Philadelphia anymore," I said.

Pete gave me a funny look. "Don't speak too soon."

"What do you mean?"

"I saw a big, black Lincoln drive into the front lot a couple of hours ago, but I didn't see who was behind the wheel."

"Hey, a lot of folks drive big, black Lincolns. They're great luxury cars and very comfortable. At least the one Tony was driving was comfortable. The kind of clientele we cater to here usually is the kind that can afford big, black Lincolns, Cadillacs, Lexuses—or is that Lexi?—Beemers, Jaguars, and all those other cars I don't have a dream of ever affording."

"Me, neither, unless I marry some rich guy," Bambi added.

"Hey, wait a minute," Pete said. "I thought you were mine."

"Pete, get real. As a lover you're great, but as marriage material, not so much. Besides, even if I marry a rich guy, I'll probably still need a lover, especially if that rich guy is old and ready to kick the bucket."

I decided not to comment. Sometimes silence is the best policy.

** ** **

On our walk from our cottage to the stables we could see the main guest parking lot. Although there were several large black cars and SUVs, none looked like one that had been driven by Papa Guido's crew. However, I wasn't close enough to see emblems and most modern SUVs have a similar shape, so I couldn't be sure.

When we reached the stable a horse trailer hitched to a pickup truck was backed in. Lizzie was coming down the lowered rear ramp leading a black mare. A man, probably the pickup driver, was standing off to one side.

"Who's the newcomer?" I called.

"Her name's Blackie," Lizzie replied. I ran into the stable building to stand by an open stall door. Bambi and Pete followed.

"Appropriate name," I said, stroking the sleek side of the animal as she was led into the stall. "She looks well taken care of."

"Yes, I'm being a bit fussy about that. If this were my own place, I'd try to pick up a few rescue animals, those that had been mistreated. However, we have rich guests who probably wouldn't want a less than perfect horse to ride, so I've been looking for only the best."

"True. We have to follow different rules than we would for ourselves."

"Were you interested in going riding this afternoon?"

"Yeah, if we can. I realize Blackie won't be ready for us to ride yet, but Honey and Spike will do just fine."

"Actually, I can ride Blackie. I rode her a couple of times at the farm where I bought her, and she's gentle as a lamb."

"Are you planning to get any more-spirited animals?"

"I don't know yet. I guess I'll have to see how our insurance policy is written. I know there are always a couple of people who like something livelier, but there's always the risk of injury, even with a gentle horse, but definitely with a spirited one. I don't like the thought of some idiot biting off more than he can chew, getting thrown, and then suing us for giving him a dangerous animal. My folks got nailed once at their own stable like that. Our insurance covered it, but our rates went up quite a bit afterward."

Lizzie left the stable building, and I heard her talking to the man by the truck while Bambi and I worked at making friends with Blackie. Pete tried to stroke her nose, but she backed away, probably not seeing him but repelled by the cold touch.

I heard the truck door slam and the motor start, and then the truck and trailer drove away. Lizzie returned to the stable.

"Come on, let's get saddled up, and we can go for a trail ride. I'm sick of riding in trucks all day." Twenty minutes later we were headed out the forest road, bound for the trail to the pond, and then beyond if Blackie didn't rebel.

We rode along at a walk, me on Honey beside Lizzie on Blackie. Bambi on Spike brought up the rear with Pete trotting alongside her. I turned my head toward Lizzie and asked, "How many more horses do you have in the pipeline?"

"Six right now. That'll give us nine, which will be enough to start letting guests ride them. The trail ride leader will need one, so that'll leave eight to rent. That's a good group size to begin."

"When do those six get here?"

"Actually, Wednesday. I expected them last week, but there was a foul-up in the paperwork. Lord, deliver us from paperwork. Those darned Egyptians invented paper, and it's haunted us ever since."

"Still, it's better than clay or stone tablets."

"Yeah, those would require some awesome filing cabinets, to say the least."

We continued to ride, mostly at a walk, because Lizzie said she wanted to let Blackie get to know the lay of the land. Also, although I didn't mention it to her, this way Pete was able to keep up. Blackie didn't put up a fuss when we passed the pond, entered the trail off the lane, crossed the paved road, and continued toward the hunter's cabin.

As we rounded a bend in the trail beyond which the cabin was visible, I noticed a black vehicle parked next to it. As we got closer, the vehicle, at this distance recognizable as a large, black SUV, backed up, turned around, and headed off along the dirt road that led away from the cabin toward civilization.

"Wasn't that one of Papa Guido's cars?" Bambi asked.

"I doubt it," I said. "What the heck would one of those be doing here? They all went back to Philly, as far as I know. Also, I'm not sure how they'd have found out about this cabin. I never mentioned it to Tony, and I doubt Liz said anything because she has nothing linking this place to the carjacking, at least nothing she can use."

"It must be frustrating being able to see and hear things that most people can't and then have to try to explain them," Lizzie said. "I'm pretty sure I believe you, but there is a smidgen of doubt."

"Yeah, that's a problem. At least on Cape Cod, Jason could see the ghosts although again he couldn't officially use what he knew. However, it gave him definite clues as to where to look for usable evidence."

When we reached the cabin, we dismounted and tied the horses to a convenient tree. I walked to the door and noticed it wasn't closed properly. "This doesn't look good," I said. "I'm sure the cops would have locked up after they left. There's some nice stuff in there; real temptation to a burglar."

"Maybe the person driving the SUV is the owner," Bambi said. "After all, there are a lot of black SUVs in the world, and I'm not sure the one that just drove away was a Lincoln. Quite a few have a similar body shape and size."

"Yeah, one shape fits all," Lizzie said.

"Well, there are differences, but they're hard to spot from a couple of hundred yards away."

"I'd like to check the interior just in case they left us a new body," I said, "but I don't want to leave fingerprints."

Lizzie held up her hands to show that she was wearing leather gloves. Then she pushed the door open.

"Won't they discover your DNA or at least horse DNA where you touched the door?" I asked.

"Why the heck would they even check for that? Fingerprints, maybe, but DNA I doubt. This ain't CSI."

"No, you're right, although if we do find a corpse in there, this area may get to look like it."

Runaway

Of course, we all followed Lizzie inside the cabin. Admittedly, if the door had been locked, maybe even latched closed, we might have refrained. No, don't be silly, Three-Zee. First, we would have had Pete walk through a wall or door to make sure nobody was lurking inside, and then we would have entered. I don't know about Lizzie's skills in that area, but Bambi can work wonders with an ordinary door lock and a bit of wire. I keep forgetting to have her teach me the technique.

Technically, I guess it's not breaking and entering because we aren't actually breaking anything, but it certainly is entering. I remember hiding in a closet on Cape Cod, but I digress.

Fortunately, nobody was home unless they were down in a hidden cellar. Been there; done that. The place was in good shape; not even dust on the furniture although the person we'd seen driving away could have been the owner or a cleaning person. Scratch the latter. I doubt most cleaners can afford a car of the type we'd just seen.

Being nosy, we opened drawers and cabinets, but nothing seemed to indicate that the place had been ransacked. If the previous visitor hadn't been the owner, he, or she, apparently wasn't there to steal whatever was available because there was some nice stuff lying around and a pretty impressive big-screen TV on the living room wall with a DVD player beneath it. I know most people don't use DVDs anymore, but without good streaming service on cable or a satellite dish, they're still an acceptable alternative. I hadn't noticed a satellite dish outside, but then I hadn't actually looked for one, either.

One thing we did discover was there was no indication of who might be the owner. We riffled through drawers, etc. However, I suppose while the police were in the process of removing Tyrone Geiger's mortal remains, they might have confiscated any identifications. At least I'm sure they searched the drawers and cabinets for information. After all, it was a crime scene, so I'm not sure whether a search warrant would have been necessary. Besides, I suspect the police occasionally might bend the rules, especially if nobody's looking.

Unenlightened, we went outside, pulling the door shut behind us and making sure it latched—no point in letting the wild critters take over the place—and untied our horses. I had just gotten myself settled in Honey's saddle when, well, I learned that Honey was not the kind of horse to work in western movies, especially the ones with a lot of gunfire. All it took was a single gunshot, and she took off like a bat out of... Well, you get the idea.

As I said earlier, I'm a fairly experienced rider, but even the best rider probably wouldn't be prepared to handle a totally spooked horse. Honey was determined to put as much distance between herself and that gunshot as she could, and she really didn't seem to care about the fact I was sitting on her back, hanging on for dear life. American Western saddles have saddle horns, primarily to tie off ropes when roping steers, but they also make great handles when the horse you're riding is in total panic mode.

All good things must come to an end, which in this case was nearly my life. Honey swerved left and my body tried to continue straight. The result was that I toppled off her right side—the wrong side, by the way, for both mounting and dismounting—was dragged for several yards until my foot slipped from the stirrup, and then blacked out.

** ** **

"I wish you'd find a better place to hang out," a voice said. I tried to open my eyes, but when I did, some sort of light above me caused a stabbing pain in my head, so I shut them again. The voice was familiar. Okay, Bambi.

I mumbled something. My fuzzy brain told me it had instructed my vocal apparatus to say, "Where am I?" but I'm not sure exactly what came out.

"They're planning to name the emergency room after you. All you need is three more visits."

"Don' get snoddy," I mumbled.

"I wonder whether a bicycle helmet would work. No, I think a motorcycle helmet would offer more protection. Cowboy hats are worthless. By the way, does it hurt?"

"Does what hurt? Oh yeah, my head. It does, kind of, and it seems to be getting worse."

"Not a surprise. You were lucky. You just missed a big rock by inches. Otherwise, well, maybe we'd be talking on a different plane."

"Like person to ghost."

"Yeah, like that."

"Could you turn off that miserable ceiling light?"

"Let me check. Yeah, there's a switch over here." The light went dark, and I opened my eyes to a much dimmer and more soothing illumination level.

"Honey spooked. How about your horse?"

"Both Spike and Blackie stood there, calm as anything. That helped because when you took your spill, we were able to reach you quickly."

"I seem to remember hearing something like a gunshot."

"Yeah, both Lizzie and I are pretty sure that's what it was. Unfortunately, that's not exactly illegal as long as the shooter wasn't aiming at a person or game that's out of season."

"Which is most at this time of year."

"Unless the shooter mistook you for a woodchuck. They're in season all the time."

"Don't they get a reprieve on Groundhog Day?"

"Only if they forecast an early spring. Otherwise, they're fair game."

** ** **

Head injuries can be dangerous, especially when the head in question has been bounced along fairly hard ground for several yards. I asked for a mirror; request denied. However, Bambi was kind enough to tell me I was either going to need a hat or a wig to cover up what I hoped would be a temporary bald spot on the back of said head. All I knew for sure was that it hurt like the dickens now that I was fully awake.

Because of the distance between Mountain Woods and East Stroudsburg, the hospital at the latter location decided to keep me for a couple of days until all danger of a concussion had passed. Also, it was now late Tuesday morning. My fall had happened Monday afternoon. Why didn't I feel more rested after all that sleep?

Bambi hung around until around eleven, but then she said she had to get back to work the afternoon shift in the kitchen. She said George had been very concerned about my condition and had actually followed the ambulance to the hospital, but this morning he was tied up in a meeting with Marvelous Marvin.

Lizzie had ridden for help because we were in a cell phone dead zone, while Bambi had remained with me. After I fell, Honey had stopped running and eventually come back to check on me, but horses aren't very helpful when it comes to providing medical care. At least we had been near a road, the lane to the cabin, so an ambulance could get in and haul me out.

Unfortunately, neither Bambi nor Lizzie had seen the shooter, and with all the commotion and the fact they were near the cabin where a sharp sound would reflect off the walls, they had no idea from which direction the sound had come. All they could agree upon was that it was loud and, therefore, probably very close.

Bambi left and I slept, probably for quite a while because I opened my eyes to a darkening sky outside a wall of windows. Either they'd replaced the ceiling lights and knocked holes in the wall, or I'd been moved from the ER to a room. I lay there half asleep until I heard a knock on what I assumed was the door to my room. I turned my head, which brought on a terrible headache, but I managed to say, "Come in, please." However, I wasn't sure it was loud enough to be heard more than about five feet from my bed.

Anyway, whether or not the person heard me, the door opened. I was expecting a nurse or other staff member, so I was somewhat surprised to see that my visitor was George.

"Three-Zee, you must stop visiting this place. Our insurance company is starting to complain."

"And a good day to you, too, George," I said, probably rather sarcastically. Fortunately, George didn't seem to be offended, not that I really cared. My head really hurt.

"I'm sorry I couldn't get here earlier. I was supposed to meet with Marvin yesterday afternoon, but he canceled at the last minute and insisted on meeting this morning."

"That's okay. It doesn't look like I'm going anywhere."

"No, and I don't expect you to, at least not until the doctors clear you. Concussion can be dangerous."

"So I've heard from nearly everybody."

"What the heck happened, anyway? Bambi tried to explain it to me, but I'm not sure I got it correctly."

"We had ridden out to that cabin in the woods, the one where we discovered that guy's body, but that wasn't why we were there. It's merely a nice trail to ride."

"Mm. Bambi said something about a gunshot."

"Yeah, we had dismounted to give the horses a bit of a rest"—I wasn't about to tell him we'd also searched the cabin—"and had just remounted when we heard what sounded like a gunshot. I can't be sure that's what it was, but it certainly sounded like it. Anyway, I was on Honey, Bambi on Spike, and Lizzie on the new horse, Blackie." George nodded. "I guess the other horses may be used to sharp, loud noises, but Honey panicked and took off. I'm usually comfortable on horseback, but I wasn't ready for something like that. She swerved, I fell off, and I guess I wound up being dragged for a bit before my foot slipped out of the stirrup. I kind of remember being dragged, and then I was lying in, I think, the ER with Bambi hovering over me."

"Well, you did give us all quite a scare. By the way, I called your mother and told her what happened. She said she'd try to get up here this coming weekend, but for the moment the store where she works is shorthanded and they don't want to let her off. I told her that as far as I knew you were doing okay, and you could have a better visit over the weekend. She can stay with me in my apartment."

"Thanks, George. Yeah, the weekend will be better. I'm not much into visitors right now anyway. Headaches and all that."

"Yes, I understand. You'd better rest. Oh, and don't worry about your job. Cathy will take care of the stuff you did. She owes you anyway from when you filled in for her last fall."

George said goodbye and headed off, probably back to the resort. I remember dozing and waking for the next couple of hours until a nurse came in for the bedtime vitals check. Supposedly, sleep is good for you, so why do hospitals insist upon waking you up every couple of hours to bother you?

In the Night

I complain about the nurses waking me to take my vitals, and at first that's what I thought was happening. However, no top-notch nurse—heck, not even a terrible nurse—takes one's vitals by holding a pillow over one's face. Somehow, I managed to push the pillow away far enough to scream. With that, the person holding it, who I'm pretty sure was not a nurse, dropped it and ran out of my room. Unfortunately, in the dim light I saw little of the person, not even enough to indicate whether my assailant was a man or a woman. I was pretty sure the person was bigger than a five-year-old, but other than that, no dice.

The nurse who answered my scream, which was probably more effective at getting her attention than a frantically activated call bell, said she hadn't noticed anyone leaving my room, but the nurse's station was farther down the hall, and from where she sat, she couldn't see the length of the hall or even the door to my room, so it was possible somebody had run out and exited the floor. She did wonder whether I might have dreamed the whole incident, but I was pretty sure I hadn't. Anyway, she did say she'd call security and have them post one of their people outside my door for a while.

The whole mess reignited my splitting headache, and I had a heck of a time getting back to sleep. Finally, the same nurse showed up with a needle, which she said contained a sedative the doctor had prescribed, and stabbed it into the little port on my IV hose. That worked. The next thing I knew, the sun was shining through my window—a bit blinding perhaps, but at least I was alive to see it.

Breakfast arrived, and I was allowed to sit on the side of my bed to eat. I still had the headache, but it had subsided to a dull throb rather than feeling like somebody was using my head to test knife blades.

I had just finished eating some fairly edible scrambled eggs when Liz Heyer walked into my room. That was a surprise, but a good one.

"I understand somebody doesn't like you," were her first words.

"Yes, and I can't understand why because I'm such a nice person. I am rather surprised to see you here, though. I'd have thought the local police would have been summoned, assuming the hospital summoned anybody beyond their own security staff."

"If it was an attempted murder—holding a pillow over somebody's face usually can be construed as that—they're required to notify the police. As it was, I was on my way down here to talk to you. I met their officer downstairs, and he decided one cop was enough, especially as he'd just received an emergency call. However, I do have to let them know what I learned, if anything."

"Why were you coming to see me, not that I mind having you here?"

"I have a few more questions about what your ghost friend remembers. However, let's take care of the gorilla in the room first."

"Gorilla in the room…?"

"Yeah, the guy with the pillow. Are you sure you didn't dream the whole thing?"

"That's what the nurse asked me last night, and no, I'm not absolutely sure. However, I'm sure she reported that she found a pillow lying on the floor next to my bed when she came in."

"I haven't spoken with her yet, but I'll be sure to ask. Okay, let's assume the incident actually happened. Did you get a good look at your assailant?"

"Heck, no. Definitely tall enough to be an adult, but I only got a glimpse of a back when the person ran out the door. I have no idea whether the person was male or female. However, I'm pretty sure it wasn't a gorilla." I grinned and she grinned back.

"Not a ghost?"

"No, like I told you, ghosts can't pick things up, and certainly they can't manipulate a pillow to suffocate somebody."

"But you don't know that for sure."

"No, I guess not. I'm only going with what I've experienced in the past."

"Okay, let's rule out ghosts, and gorillas, too. Who did you piss off lately?"

"Probably a lot of people, but I don't think anybody enough to want to kill me."

"Yeah, that's what most victims say. You'd be surprised how nasty some people can become over the smallest incidents."

I nodded, but that started my head hurting again.

"I'll report to the local cops that you have no idea who might have done this. What did the nurse do with the pillow she found on the floor?"

"I think she picked it up and put it over there on the chair, but again, I'm not sure."

"No, and she's already gone home or wherever, so I can't ask her. Those CSI shows always deal with perfectly preserved evidence, something we rarely get. I'd take that pillow for forensic analysis, but it's doubtful there's anything on there that could be used as evidence unless you'd managed to bite the perp and they'd left a few bloodstains."

"No such luck as far as I know."

"That's what I thought."

"What kind of questions did you have for me that brought you here in the first place?"

"Are your ghost friends still hanging around?"

"Other than Pete, who's more or less a permanent fixture, no. Lauren and little Johnny faded away last weekend after they found out who was responsible for their accident. I don't know whether they'll be back, but I've never experienced that in the past, so I rather think it's a one-way trip."

"Which is why your friend, Pete, hasn't faded away."

"Yeah, he really does like Bambi, so I'm pretty sure he's afraid if he fades away, he'll never see her again. Of course, there's a possibility he'll see her after she dies at some point in the future, but I think he's working on the bird-in-the-hand theory."

"Worth two in the bush."

"Something like that. Besides, even if he could catch up with her in the afterlife, by then she might have been married or, at least, committed to somebody else."

"Did Lauren remember any more about the kidnapping?"

"No, or at least if she did, she didn't mention it. I'm afraid what I told you is all I know."

"What were you doing out there by the cabin where you found Tyrone Geiger's body?"

"We'd gone for a ride, and that's a rather nice trail, wide enough for horses with no major obstacles. Did Lizzie or Bambi fill you in on what happened?"

"They said you heard a gunshot, which spooked your horse. Unfortunately, even if we find the shooter, they didn't actually do anything wrong because it's private property and target shooting is legal. Of course, if they were shooting at people or any animals that were out of season, that would be a different thing."

"Did they mention the SUV?"

"What SUV?"

"Shortly before we arrived at the cabin a black SUV pulled away from the side and drove away toward the highway."

"Mm, no. Did you get a good look at it?"

"Other than that it was big and black, no. We were too far away to see details. Oh, and another thing. The cabin door was slightly ajar."

"It was locked this morning when I drove out there."

"Yeah, well, we pulled it shut and made sure it was locked."

"After you'd gone inside and searched the place."

"Er, well, maybe, or maybe not. We were afraid if the door wasn't closed properly, some squirrels or chipmunks or whatever might get inside and make a mess. Maybe even a bear."

"Or lions or tigers. Okay, as long as you didn't damage or steal anything, I guess I won't try to charge you. You were just being a good Samaritan."

"Yeah, that. Did you ever find out more about the owner or owners?"

"No more than what I told you. I guess the hunting club doesn't have an official address, and nobody seems to know who they are. Tax bills go to a post office box, and the taxes are paid up to date, so there's no reason for the taxing bodies to investigate farther. The checks used to pay the taxes come from a law firm, but they're claiming attorney-client privilege. Apparently, none of their partners or staff are owners of the property."

"Can't you get a court order?"

"We're trying, but things like that don't happen quickly, if ever. We're still trying to track down a next of kin for Tyrone Geiger."

"Don't they have any information in their records from his carjacking conviction?"

"No next of kin listed. Maybe he was all alone in the world."

"I feel sad for him. However, that's no reason to become a carjacker."

"No, I guess not. Still, it's cheaper than actually buying or renting a car."

"Unless you get caught."

"Yeah, unless that."

My headache seemed to be getting worse, so I lay back on the bed. Liz lent a hand by pushing the button to raise the head.

"Getting back to that attempted murder," Liz said, "why do you think you might have been targeted?"

"I really have no idea. As I said, I'm pretty sure ghosts can't do it, and I don't think anybody has me on their hit list. Hm. Maybe something about the cabin?"

"But why? It's merely a cabin in the woods, and there are no signs warning people away. Of course, you were trespassing on private property, but even then the owner doesn't have the right to come after you and try to kill you."

"Tell that to Abner Whitelaw," I muttered.

"Who?"

"Abner Whitelaw, the guy who took potshots with his shotgun at anybody who got too close to his lakefront property, including Bambi and me."

"Oh yeah, I heard about that. However, as far as I know, he's still locked up. I think we'd have been notified if he'd escaped or even been released on parole."

"Probably."

Possible Perps

"So, who do you think knows about you and your friends visiting the cabin, assuming that's the reason you're being targeted?"

"Okay, of course there are Bambi and Lizzie, but I really don't suspect either of them, Bambi because she's been my best friend forever, and Lizzie because she had plenty of other opportunities to kill me and no particular reason as far as I know."

"Still, she could have been the one to spook your horse, hoping you'd fall off, which you did, and be killed, which you weren't."

"True on all counts, but I think either Bambi or I would have seen her fire a gun or even light and throw a firecracker."

"Yeah, I was just offering options. Who else?"

"I guess a number of people at the resort. George, certainly, and Cathy, maybe. I'm not sure about other employees or any of the guests. I haven't said much about it, but it's possible Bambi or Lizzie has. The only other person I can think of at the moment is Luke Walker."

"I'm assuming you aren't misnaming the character from *Star Wars*, so who is he?"

"Yeah, he said that happens all the time. He's the brother of Harry Walker, one of our support staff who at this time of year takes care of the boat rentals. Luke just started working for the resort as a lifeguard. We met him one day when he was out for a run, and we told him about the good trail to the cabin."

"Would he have any reason to bear you any animosity? I mean, could he be avenging some sort of thing you did to his brother?"

"Not as far as I know. Harry's been there longer than I have, and we've always gotten along quite well. Admittedly, I'm now more or less their boss, but I haven't sensed any resentment, at least not on Harry's part. Luke, well, I don't know, but I've only talked to him a couple of times, and I've never given him any orders."

"It's possible he resents the fact you were promoted to Assistant Activities Director over his brother."

"I guess, but I never sensed Harry wanted any sort of management position." I thought for a moment. "There is one thing, though."

"Oh? What?"

"Luke is a great shot, so I'm told. I guess he competes."

"So, it's possible he fired the shot that spooked your horse."

"I guess, but why he'd be out there at the cabin firing a gun beats me. I didn't check whether he was working at the time. Maybe it was whoever was driving that black SUV we saw driving away."

"Unfortunately, black SUVs, even big ones, are fairly common beasts. I see quite a few parked in the resort parking lot when I come there, even a couple in the employee lot although those are less spectacular and a bit more worn looking."

"Yeah, Marvelous Marvin drives one, and the goons who drove Papa Guido and his crew did, too."

"I assume Papa Guido is Guido Corsana, but who the heck is Marvelous Marvin?"

"Marvin Pendergast. Along with George and several others, he's one of the owners of Mountain Woods. He's also a total pain in the ass."

"I'm guessing he's staying at the resort right now."

"Yeah, he showed up the day before Papa Guido did and had insisted on the bridal suite, which was appropriately refurnished for a non-bridal party. However, Papa Guido was a paying guest, and paying guests get priority over non-paying owners."

"Which I assume Marvelous Marvin didn't appreciate."

"Not in the least. However, I had nothing whatever to do with that. He did come into Cathy's office one day complaining about… Come to think of it, I can't really remember what he was complaining about, but then he complains about everything."

"Did he get back into the suite he wanted after Mr. Corsana's party departed?"

"In a heartbeat. I guess he's still there. Anyway, he was yesterday because George was complaining about him last evening."

"And he'd have no reason to want you out of the way?"

"Not as far as I can figure. Oh, Pete did say he thought he saw one of Papa Guido's cars in our parking lot Monday, which is odd because they all left for Philadelphia on Saturday."

"What's odd about those cars that Pete would recognize one of them?"

"Nothing, really. A lot of wealthy people stay at Mountain Woods, and a lot of them drive big, black SUVs including Lincolns like Papa Guido's crew. Pete didn't see who was driving, so it could have been almost anybody."

"Does Marvelous Marvin drive a Lincoln, too?"

I thought for a moment. "No, I think it's a Jag, but I could be wrong. Anyway, it's big and black. So, Audi, Jag, Lincoln, Cadillac, Range Rover, or others too numerous to mention."

"And the one you saw by the cabin?"

"Any or none of the above. We were really too far away to see the brand or condition. For all I can remember, it could have been an older black Honda or Toyota."

"I'll ask Lizzie and Bambi. Maybe they noticed more."

"Yeah, it's possible, I guess."

Liz got up to leave. "Have they given you any idea as to when you might be kicked out of here?"

"Not yet. I know the doctor seemed quite concerned about my headaches." I grimaced because mine seemed to be getting worse. "I remember him saying something about a brain scan."

"What happens if they don't find one?"

"Find what?"

"A brain." Liz laughed.

"There are days I'm pretty sure they won't find one."

"I have days like that, too," Liz said. Then she headed out of the room, and I settled back to await my fate and enjoy my headache.

** ** **

Computer-aided tomography or CAT or CT scans are fairly simple. First, they inject you with some kind of dye—I was rather hoping I wouldn't turn purple or green—and then they make you lie on this hard table, which I'm sure contains pipes full of freezing liquid. Finally, they pass you back and forth through this giant doughnut, asking you to hold your breath briefly at times. It's easy enough; much quicker and quieter than a brain-scan MRI, or so I'm told.

After the scan you're wheeled back to your room where you wait, ostensibly until somebody who can figure out what they're looking at "reads" the scan and then informs your doctor. That can take anywhere from several minutes to several hours depending upon the availability of both the reader and the doctor. Meanwhile, you wait, hoping that you didn't flunk the test.

I was lying in my bed dozing after my gourmet dinner—edible roast turkey with mashed potatoes and rather plasticky gravy and a side of mushy overcooked broccoli followed by tapioca pudding for dessert, mostly as good as the food we were served in the resort's employee dining room—when Bambi walked into my room followed by Pete.

"Are they going to spring you from this prison?" Bambi asked.

"Don't know. Still waiting for the CAT scan results."

"Where did they send them for analysis? India?"

"Probably. Did Liz Heyer see you?"

"Yeah, she wanted to know whether I could give her more info about that SUV we saw pulling away from the cabin, but I really didn't get a good look. I guess she was going to ask Lizzie, too."

"That's what she told me. We had a pretty long chat this morning, but I can't think of anybody who might want to hurt me."

"Hurt you. Hell, they wanted to kill you. There is a difference, you know."

"I know."

"Being dead isn't all that bad," Pete said, turning from reading various notices on the room's bulletin board.

"I suppose not, but there seem to be drawbacks, too."

"Like…"

"Eating foods you like, sex, sleeping, … stuff like that."

"Yeah, I guess you living folks might consider those to be drawbacks. However, you don't have to worry about pain, hunger, thirst, or dying."

"True, but what happens after you move on?"

"Good point. I have no idea."

At that moment a nurse walked into the room. "The doctor will be stopping by in a few minutes," she said, glancing at Bambi but totally ignoring Pete, who was standing more or less in front of her.

"Does he have my test results?"

"I believe so. I just wanted to make sure you were in your room."

"Where else would I be?"

"You're right. There is the bathroom, though, and you are allowed to walk in the halls with a walker."

"Nobody told me that."

"Oh, well, you are."

"Thanks. I'll think about it. How about horseback riding?"

The nurse gave me a startled look. "Not in here. Anyway, weren't you thrown from a horse? Isn't that why you're here?"

"Yes to both questions."

The nurse shook her head and left us to go annoy somebody else. Bambi sat on a chair by my bedside, and Pete stood in the corner.

"Aren't you afraid somebody will try to kill you again after you get home from the hospital?" Pete asked.

"Yes, but what can I do about it? I can't stay here indefinitely, and this place has proven not to be particularly safe anyway. I doubt George is going to spring for an armed guard outside the cottage twenty-four seven. I guess I'll just have to take my chances."

"Maybe you could move to a room in the employee dorm," Bambi suggested. "That might be more secure than the cottage."

"And leave you two to get up to all kinds of shenanigans in the cottage."

"Well, yeah, we sort of have been enjoying the privacy since you've been in here."

"That's what I figured. Instead of an armed guard, what you two need is a live-in chaperone."

The doctor walked into the room then, probably cutting off any witty remark either Bambi or Pete was planning to make. He had a somewhat concerned look on his face, which made my stomach take a few flips, or maybe it was the crappy gravy on that turkey. He ignored Pete, meaning he probably wasn't aware of his presence.

"How are you feeling, Miss Zook?" he asked.

I'm not particularly fussy about what people call me, but "Miss Zook" somehow makes me feel like an old-maid schoolteacher. However, rather than making a fuss, I merely answered his question. "I still have a headache, if that's what you mean?"

"Yes, you probably will for another day or two. Fortunately, the brain swelling you're experiencing is mild and appears to be shrinking from the CT scan we did yesterday, so I'm going to release you tomorrow morning. You shouldn't drive until I see you again, so will you have somebody available to take you home?"

I looked at Bambi, who said, "Yeah, I can come down. Fred won't be happy, but he'll manage without me for a couple of hours." Fred Kingston is our head chef.

"What time?" I asked.

"Hard to say," the doctor replied. "After I release you, you'll have to go through that whole paperwork thing. I expect to be doing my rounds after about ten, so I'd say get here between ten and eleven." Bambi nodded.

"How about restrictions other than driving?" I asked.

"I'll go over them in the morning, but I'd say you should rest a lot, be careful not to bump your head, and don't go horseback riding. Okay, eventually you'll be able to do it again, but please wear a helmet. Cowboy hats aren't much protection."

"Except from the sun."

"Yes, that, of course, but not for hitting your head."

"Football or motorcycle?" Bambi asked.

"Huh?"

"What kind of helmet?"

"Oh, even a bicycle helmet would be better than nothing, but definitely not just a soft hat or bareheaded."

Home Again, More or Less

Hospitals are notorious for announcing that you'll be leaving shortly, where "shortly" means within the next twelve hours or so. After the doctor stops by for a final checkup and then announces you're being released, a nurse eventually comes into your room to explain your restrictions as well as your next appointment date at the doctor's office. Then you wait while some mysterious things happen about which you have no idea whatsoever, probably waiting for authorization from God and three higher-ups. Bambi and Pete showed up at ten-fifteen, shortly after the doctor left my room, so those other steps still had to take place. It was nearly twelve-thirty by the time a patient transporter showed up with a wheelchair to take me down to the entrance where Bambi was to meet me with her truck.

Riding in Bambi's old pickup is jarring to a completely healthy person, so it was pretty much sheer torture for somebody with a headache recovering from a concussion. However, we made it back to the resort with me only half dead. When we got there, Bambi pulled up outside the employee dorm.

"I presume you're implying that I'm staying here for the moment," I said.

"I checked with George last night, and he definitely agreed that this would be safer for you than down in our cottage. After they find the perp who tried to smother you, then the cottage will be okay, but not now."

"And if they never find him?"

"Or her. Anyway, Lizzie moved into her new apartment in the stables yesterday, which left her space open. Also, one of the housekeeping staff quit Monday, so her slot was open, too. George consolidated the two remaining people into the same room—fortunately, they're friends, so they didn't kick up a fuss—which gives you a luxurious room all to yourself."

"Bam, these rooms are adequate but hardly luxurious."

"I know, but I'm practicing to become a public relations person."

"In other words, a professional liar."

"Something like that. I'm sorry I don't have a wheelchair to transport you to your room, which is on the third floor. Thank heavens we have an elevator."

** ** **

The employee residence building or dorm, three-stories high, is behind and connected to the main resort building by a series of hallways that provide access to the various management offices, the kitchens, and the employee dining room. Guests are normally not permitted in those hallways unless accompanied by an appropriate employee for necessary purposes, such as visiting George's office.

I was walking slowly beside Bambi in the main hallway of the dorm heading for the elevator when Marvin Pendergast came flying around the corner where this hallway connected with one to the dining room. I use the term "flying" because the man always seemed to be walking extremely fast when he wasn't standing yelling at somebody. As it was, he nearly knocked me down, gave me a dirty look as if to say I should know better than to be in his way, and then tooled on toward the parking lot. As he pushed open the door to head outside, he turned around, stopped, and stared at me, maybe realizing for the first time who I was, if he even remembered. Then he frowned and resumed his breakneck pace into the parking lot. I wondered whether he was annoyed by Bambi's truck parked just outside the door, but when I checked with Bambi later, at least he hadn't let the air out of her tires.

It's amazing how tired one feels after a prolonged stay—okay, slightly less than two days—in the hospital. I suppose it was some aftereffect from the concussion. Still, I guess it's better to be tired than dead, even if Pete does tend to play up the virtues of being deceased. Once we were inside the elevator, a slow-moving monster that's oversized for the convenience of moving various furnishings into and out of the rooms, I sagged against the rail that encircled the area except for the doors. At the third floor, I struggled to get moving to the point where Bambi had to keep a finger pressed against the "Door Open" button until I was able to exit. Fortunately, my room was only the third one down the hall from the elevator because I probably wouldn't have been able to make it much farther.

Each room has two beds because mostly the rooms are shared. Having this one all to myself, I chose the bed closest to the window, which gave me a lovely view over the employee parking lot. However, that at least was better than looking at a blank wall or air-conditioning vents, and the woods in the distance were leafing out nicely so the view wasn't all bad. If I looked to the right, I could see the loading docks where delivery trucks backed in although none was currently parked there.

"Will you be okay here for now?" Bambi asked. "I really must get down to the kitchen, or Fred will be sharpening a knife to throw at me when I come through the door."

"He threw when I came through—ain't English wonderful?"

"Oh, shut up. If you can come up with lines like that, you're not really sick at all. I'll see you later if I duck quickly enough." Bambi left the room and me to my devices, which were to flop on the bed and take a nap.

** ** **

The sky was darkening when I opened my eyes, which meant it had to be at least seven-thirty, but at least I felt more rested. However, the sound of somebody clearing their throat probably cut three or four years off my life.

"Who the heck…?" I rolled the other way to see Cathy Schwartz sitting on the other bed. "You scared the crap out of me," I said.

"Sorry, I didn't mean to. I guess I'd be nervous, too, if somebody had tried to smother me in my sleep."

"You weren't the one, were you?"

"No. I'd probably use something like arsenic, usually slower, but harder to trace. Smothering means you have to hang around until the person's dead."

"Mm. Thanks for the reassurance. So, what brings you to my humble abode, and for that matter, how the heck did you get in? I'm assuming Bambi locked the door after herself when she left."

"Yes, but I had one of the maids let me in with her housekeeping badge."

"So, now I must fear a rogue maid, too."

"I'm afraid so, but I doubt that's who tried to kill you in the hospital."

"Have the cops been asking questions?"

"Yes, they've been wandering all over the place asking people where they were last night. I assume there's some order to their approach, but I don't see it."

"Probably we aren't meant to. Are you planning to dock my pay until I can come back to work?"

"Of course not. We just want you to get better. Besides, if I piss you off and you quit, I'll have to lead the hikes by myself. That's really not my cup of tea, but you seem to enjoy it."

"Yeah, I've always been a sort of outdoors person. I'd even be willing to help Lizzie lead trail rides."

"Speaking of Lizzie, she was wondering whether it would be okay to visit you."

"Of course, as long as she isn't planning to smother me. Cathy, I have no idea who might have it in for me. I mean, I guess I occasionally tick somebody off—heck, we all do—but to make them so mad they'd want to kill me? No, that doesn't make sense."

"Maybe somebody thinks you know something they don't think you should."

"Yeah, but what, and who?"

"I remember back in school they spoke about the six w's: who, what, where, when, why, and how? Okay, we know the how, but we're kind of weak on the other five."

At that moment we heard a knock on the door. Cathy opened it to admit Lizzie and Bambi.

After sharing the usual greetings and how are you's, Bambi said, "I requested that my key card be activated for your room as well as the cottage." The resort has installed electronic key card readers on all doors so that individual keys can be activated to open any or all of them. Of course, "all doors" is extremely restricted. I think George has that access as well as maintenance, but I'm not really sure about them. Maybe access for maintenance is given only as needed.

"That's good. I guess I have to trust you. Besides, why would you want to kill me, unless you secretly harbor a desire to own Snickers."

"Nobody owns Snickers, or any other cat for that matter," Bambi said.

"True." By now I was sitting up in bed. Bambi and Lizzie sat in the two chairs, and Cathy had again taken a seat on the other bed. I was rather surprised Pete hadn't come with Bambi, but I wasn't about to ask his whereabouts.

"Of course, you do snore…"

"I do not." I looked at Lizzie. "How are you going to handle Honey's aversion to gunshots?"

"I'm not sure yet. That's something I hadn't checked for when I chose the horses, but now I'm going to check each one. They can be trained out of it, but it does take a bit of time. I'm not sure how many gunshots the horses are going to be exposed to, and car engines backfiring is pretty much a thing of the past, but I'm sure there are other sharp noises that might spook them. I guess some of our guests wouldn't be afraid to sue if their horse bolted."

"I think some of them have their lawyers on speed dial. By the way, you aren't mad at me about something, are you?"

Lizzie looked startled. "No, why?"

"I'm just trying to figure out who'd want to kill me."

"No, not me, although you really do have to stop falling off my horses. It kind of scares them."

"Yeah, I can see that it might. I understand Honey came back to check on me."

"Yes, she did, and she really looked worried about it."

"Lizzie, how does a horse look worried?"

"I don't know. It's just something I sense. Oh, by the way, that new guy, what's his name, Luke Skywalker or something like that, was down by the stables. I see him out running quite a bit."

"Luke Walker," I corrected.

"He does seem quite athletic," Cathy said, "but he's a good lifeguard, or at least he's always at the pool when he's supposed to be there."

"Yes, but we won't know about his lifeguarding skills until he actually saves a life. I wonder whether he's keeping up with his shooting skills."

"I don't know, but those probably won't help with his lifeguarding."

"No, unless he decides to shoot the person in trouble in the water because then they won't drown."

"Hm, that probably wouldn't go over well with our guests, either," Cathy said.

"So, what now?"

"Well, we could wait until the next attempt on your life," Bambi said.

"Yeah, that's okay if somebody's stationed outside my door twenty-four seven, but what if that person has to pee or something?"

"You're right. Somebody could easily smother you while your guard is taking a pee. Two guards, maybe?"

"I doubt George will spring for one guard, let alone two."

"He is kind of planning to marry your mother, so he probably wouldn't want his stepdaughter to join his stepson."

"You mean dead."

"Yeah, that."

Gone, but Where?

Hi! I'm Bambi Bamberger. You may be wondering why I'm suddenly the narrator of this story, especially as I'm pretty sure Three-Zee will criticize my writing skills after she reads this, assuming she ever does. Well, it's like this.

Last evening Cathy, Lizzie, and I hung out in Three-Zee's room until after nine, but then we all left her, partially because she was really getting sleepy and complaining about her headache again, and partially because the rest of us have jobs that require us to be well-rested and perky in the morning. Okay, perky may be pushing things, but with enough coffee…

Anyway, this morning prior to heading to the kitchen to begin my breakfast shift at six, I fed Snickers, cleaned his litter box, and decided to make a quick stop at Three-Zee's room. I was surprised to find the door unlocked because I had made doubly sure it was locked prior to returning to the cottage last evening, and it was way too early for housekeeping to be making any rounds. They do tend to hit the employee rooms prior to the guest rooms in order not to disturb any guests who might be late sleepers—employees don't count—but nobody harasses even the employees prior to about seven.

I opened the door quietly so as not to disturb Three-Zee, who I figured might still be sleeping. But she wasn't. She wasn't even in bed. Her bathroom door was closed, but I opened it after there was no response to my knock and call, and she wasn't in there, either. Her pajamas were lying in a heap on her unmade bed, so I hoped she hadn't gone roaming in her birthday suit. However, her phone was still connected to its charger on her nightstand, an ominous sign.

I hurried downstairs to the employee dining room where quite a few early-shift people, mostly housekeeping staff at this hour, were chowing down, but nobody admitted to seeing her. After a quick check of the parking lot where her beat-up old car sat undisturbed, I hurried to her office. Nobody. I stuck my nose into the kitchen to alert Fred that I might be a few minutes late, and then I ran to the stables. Lizzie was up and feeding the horses, now numbering six, but she said she hadn't seen Three-Zee, either.

I had been worried before, but I was really worried now. Had she gone walkabout, as the Australians might say, or had somebody decided to kidnap her. Either option wasn't good. Could she have gone into a confused state—I wasn't completely comfortable with those recurring headaches—and wandered off somewhere, perhaps somewhere on the lakeside trail or another trail she liked to walk, or had somebody managed to enter her room and haul her off, probably sedated because I'm sure any screams would have alerted at least one of the neighbors? Those rooms aren't all *that* soundproof.

Returning to the lodge, I popped into the security office and explained the situation. Sal was there preparing to begin his daily rounds, so he accessed the key system and discovered Three-Zee's door had been opened slightly after midnight, but no key was used, meaning Three-Zee had opened it from the inside. It opened again a half-hour later, but then not again until I'd entered a bit before six. Unlike the guest room doors that cannot be unlocked and left that way, our employee rooms do have that option.

Unfortunately, this information gave me a time but not whether Three-Zee had gone off on her own or whether somebody had escorted her out, probably against her will. To add to the difficulty, the surveillance camera in that hallway was out of order waiting for a replacement. After leafing through other camera images, Sal finally managed to find one that showed Three-Zee in the north stairwell with somebody about ten feet behind her. Three-Zee seemed to be walking okay and not staggering, which she might have been if she had suffered some sort of medical emergency. The camera outside the exit door showed her again, again with somebody about ten feet behind her, but whether that person was with her or merely traveling in the same direction was impossible to tell. Also, that person's image wasn't clear enough to make out exactly who it was. There's a pole-mounted camera in the employee parking lot, but it was aimed away from the building, and the recording from just after Three-Zee left the building didn't show her or the other person.

"So, what do we do now, Sal?" I asked.

"I have to be careful because I can't go around accusing somebody if I don't have at least some kind of reason."

"I know, but Three-Zee has disappeared. Isn't that reason enough?"

"No, not for twenty-four hours. She's an adult and as such has the right to her privacy."

"I understand, but she's suffering from concussion and was nearly murdered the other night. Aren't they reasons enough?"

"I'll call the police, but in the absence of noticeable coercion—that other person in the stairwell wasn't exactly dragging her or even particularly close to her—I'm not sure they can do anything, either."

"Well, it's worth a try. I must get to the kitchen, but let me know whether you find out anything."

"I will, Bambi. I certainly don't want anything to happen to her, either."

** ** **

It was an hour later when Pete, whom I'd left hanging out with Snickers in the cottage, showed his face in the kitchen where he likes to stand around, watch me, and make snide remarks about some of the other line cooks, which they can't hear. "So, how are things going this exciting morning?" he asked.

I looked around to see whether anybody else was in earshot—holding a conversation with plain air might have drawn some unwanted attention—and then said softly, "Three-Zee's gone missing."

"How? Where?"

"Darned if I know. I went to her room…"

"Is everything okay, Bambi? I thought I heard you talking to somebody." Fred's voice. He must have come up behind me.

"Just to myself. I do that a lot."

"Oh, okay, but you know what they say."

"What's that?"

"Talking to yourself is fine. Answering yourself isn't."

"Especially if you give yourself wrong answers," I said.

Fred laughed. "Yeah, especially that."

Pete had backed away when Fred approached me. It's not that Fred could see or hear him, but he didn't want to cause any consternation by having Fred get into the same space and feel the sudden chill.

After Fred had walked away, probably to bother one of the other cooks, Pete came back. "So, what are you going to do?"

"I don't know. Sal checked the door-lock records, and it looks like she left her room around twelve-thirty. A camera shows her in the north stairwell with somebody following about ten feet behind her, and then the exit camera shows both of them going out into the parking lot. Unfortunately, we couldn't tell who the other person was or even whether they were following her. Also, the lot camera wasn't aimed toward the door, so it didn't show her after she left the building."

"And she didn't take her car?"

"No, it's still parked where it was."

"Do you think she ran away on her own?"

"No, but concussions can have strange results. She could have wandered off not even realizing what she was doing. It would be sort of like those people suffering from dementia who are found wandering around miles from home."

"Or even worse, not found, at least not until it's too late."

"Yeah, that's what worries me."

"Is there a camera watching the main entrance road to the resort?"

"I don't know. I never thought to ask Sal. However, what good would that do?"

"If a car drove out within a few minutes of Three-Zee leaving the building, it might be carrying her."

"Yes, I suppose so, but it could merely be an innocent guest or employee leaving the premises. If that person behind Three-Zee was an employee going home from work, they could be the one in that car."

"Mm. Still, it might give us a lead. Anyway, I'll take a walk around the lake just to make sure she isn't hanging out somewhere along that trail. That's the one she walks most frequently."

** ** **

The breakfast kitchen crew gets off at one-thirty after preparing lunch and then helping to precook for dinner. Most people who've never worked in a commercial kitchen such as for a restaurant or diner don't realize how much preparation work goes into those delicious, or maybe not so delicious, items that magically appear within a few minutes of being ordered. Think about how long it takes to prepare something from scratch at home, and then consider that if you had to wait that long after ordering, you'd leave long before you were served. For example, most pastas take ten or more minutes to boil to al dente, but if they're parboiled to within a minute or so of being done, they can be refrigerated and then merely immersed in boiling water for that minute or two to heat them and finish the cooking process. Only those things that can't be precooked are prepared at the last minute—think steak done as you like or most types of fried eggs.

As soon as I finished, I headed for the security office, but Sal was out somewhere and the door was locked. Cathy and George were nowhere to be seen, either. In frustration, I walked to the stables. At least Lizzie might be there and provide a sympathetic shoulder to cry on, figuratively, of course. When I got there I discovered Pete sitting on a bench outside the building.

"Did you find anything?"

"Not a thing. Okay, a few ducks and a couple of geese on the lake, and several rabbits and squirrels, but no Three-Zee. There were several rowboats and one canoe—guys fishing from the rowboats and two people paddling along in the canoe—but nobody who even vaguely resembled her."

"Is Lizzie around?"

"She just rode off on one of the new horses, but I'm not sure of the animal's name."

"Probably not important. Did she say when she'd be back?"

"Remember, she can't see me, so she doesn't know I'm here. Unless she's in the habit of announcing her plans aloud to the horses, I doubt she'd have mentioned it."

"Mm. I guess you could have given her a chill."

"No, sweetheart, I reserve those thrills for you."

Planning a Search

While I sat on the bench next to Pete waiting for Lizzie to return, which I hoped would be soon, I decided to call Liz Heyer, our state cop friend. I wondered whether Sal had called the cops as he said he would, and I wondered whether they'd be able to do anything. I hoped Liz would be available and not just settling down to sleep after an all-nighter. Fortunately, she answered on the third ring and didn't sound groggy from sleep.

"Hey, Bambi, what's up?" Liz said, much perkier than I thought she'd be.

"Er, you don't know?"

"Don't know what?"

"About Three-Zee."

"What about Three-Zee? Don't tell me somebody tried to smother her again."

"No, but Sal said he'd call to notify the police she'd gone missing."

"I hadn't heard anything, but then I don't always if it's not a case I'm assigned to. I was involved with that attempt at the hospital, but it's been moved to the detective bureau, so they're probably the ones who got the notice. Anyway, what happened?"

"We're not sure exactly. I left her at a little past nine, and I'm sure the door was locked when I went out. However, this morning at a little before six I stopped by her room to check on her. The door was unlocked, and she was nowhere to be seen."

"Could she have gone out somewhere like to the bathroom or something?"

"No, her room has a private bath, and she definitely wasn't in it. Some rooms share a bath, but even then they don't have to go out into the hall. Also, her pajamas were on the bed. I checked the dining room, her office, the stables, which is where I am now, and I even had Sal check some of the security camera footage. We discovered her going down the north stairs at about twelve-thirty with somebody—the image wasn't clear enough to tell who—about ten feet behind her. The camera outside the door caught both of them coming out, too, but again not together. Unfortunately, the parking lot camera wasn't aimed that way. The way it was aimed, it wouldn't have caught a car leaving the lot, but her car's parked where it had been anyway. I had to go to work then. Pete suggested I have Sal check the entry road camera, but Sal's not around right now. Also, Pete took a walk around the lake while I was working, but he didn't see anything."

"Are you finished with work now?"

"Yes. Nobody I could ask for help was around up at the lodge, so I came down here to see whether Lizzie had seen anything more. Unfortunately, she's out for a ride, too."

"I'll check into the reports. I'm out on patrol now, but I'll be finished in an hour or so. Officially, if you saw her leave the building of her own volition, there's not much we can do, at least not for a day or so. However, I can probably bend the rules a bit considering what she's just been through. I'm rather surprised one of the detectives hasn't contacted somebody there about it."

"It's possible they did, but as I said, I was working in the kitchen, and I haven't been able to find Sal or Cathy or George to ask them."

"Okay, I'll get back to you as soon as I can. Is your phone charged?"

"Yeah, I had it on overnight."

"Good. Wait for my call."

** ** **

I was about ready to head back to the lodge when I heard a horse whinny from somewhere off to my left and an answering whinny from the stables building, which was to my right. A few moments later Lizzie came riding out of the woods mounted on a chestnut mare. "Do you like her?" Lizzie asked as she pulled the horse to a stop in front of me. "Her name's Annabelle."

"Nice looking animal. How is she to ride?"

"Quite gentle and friendly. However, I want to give her that gunshot test. So far, Honey's the only one who spooks." Liz dismounted. Holding the reins in her right hand, she said, "Have you found Three-Zee yet?"

"No, nothing so far." I filled her in on what we'd discovered from the video cameras. "Pete said we should check for a car leaving the lot shortly after she and that other person went outside, but it could be merely an innocent guest or employee."

"Yes, of course, but the car could have Three-Zee in it, too. If her own car and your truck are in the lot, I doubt she stole another one, but she could have been a passenger, willing or unwilling." Lizzie began to lead Annabelle into the stables, and I got up to follow. "Have you notified the police?"

"Sal said he would. I called Liz Heyer a few minutes ago. She said she hadn't heard anything, but it's no longer her case, so she might not. She's going to check and then take it from there."

"Can they do anything like mount a search party?"

"Apparently, not yet. She didn't seem to be being coerced when she left the building, so she has a right to go off on her own."

"Yeah, I can see that, I guess. Still, you'd think the fact somebody just tried to murder her would weigh into their decision."

"That's was Liz's thought, too, but I guess they have rules they must follow. Anyway, she said she'd call me back in a little bit to let me know what she can do."

** ** **

A little bit turned out to be an hour and a half. I had sat with Lizzie in her new apartment—quite nice, I might add—for the first hour, but when Liz hadn't called me back by then, I decided to return to the lodge to try to locate Sal and have him check the camera recording.

Sal had just returned to his office. "Yes, I can check that camera. It's the only road into or out of the resort, so it should show if anybody drove out." He started fiddling with the security system computer as he had done earlier. "Okay, I see nobody leaving the property during that time frame. These recordings are motion sensitive to reduce the amount of recorded data, so the last car left at twelve-twenty, a few minutes before we saw Three-Zee leave the building, and then there was nothing either coming or going until one-eleven. Of course, it's possible that car contained Three-Zee, but that was at least a half hour after she went outside."

"Is there any other way out?"

"By road, not really. Okay, there is the forest road, the one we used for the hayrides last fall, but there's a locked gate at the end."

"Is that on the electronic lock system?"

"No, it's merely a simple padlock. I'm not sure who all has a key, but even then it's not a special kind of lock, so somebody could easily get a copy at a hardware store. A car could have driven out that way."

"Is there a camera on that road?"

"No, no real need. I guess we could install one, but those things are expensive, especially since you'd have to run cable for power and video and either bury them or somehow string them on poles or maybe trees, and I guess management never considered one there to be essential."

"Did you notify the police?"

"Yes, of course, as soon as I left you this morning. I haven't heard back, though."

"Did you notify Cathy and George?"

"I did as soon as it made sense. I called George in his apartment, and I saw Cathy in the hall when she was on her way to her office. I'm not sure what they can do, though."

"Probably not much more than we've already done. I have an idea. Could we check every room's access information to see who might have left their room around that time? Maybe we could use that at least to identify who might have been on the stairs with Three-Zee."

"I don't think we can without a search warrant. We'd be invading people's personal privacy. If the police show up with a warrant, that's different, but I can't just go trolling for information. The public hallways and entryways are okay, but people's room doors would be too much."

"It's unfortunate that hallway camera on Three-Zee's floor is out of order."

"Yeah, it certainly is."

** ** **

Liz showed up at about three-forty-five, now off shift. She'd called to find out where I'd be, and then joined me at the cottage where I'd gone to check on Snickers.

"Apparently the detective bureau was notified early this morning, probably by Sal shortly after you were with him, but their hands are a bit tied."

"That twenty-four-hour thing."

"Yeah. If Three-Zee had been tight up against the other person or obviously being forced along, it would be a whole different thing. However, from what Sal said, she was merely walking along on her own. The other person probably was merely following the same route. I guess it's not a particularly seldom-used way."

"No, especially for folks who don't want to wait for the elevator, which is kind of slow. Still, couldn't that person have been holding a gun on her concealed in such a way that it wouldn't be visible on the video?"

"I suppose so. Do people know about those cameras?"

"Yes, they're not concealed or anything. The ones in the main hotel are those little black blobs on the ceiling in most cases, but in the non-public areas they're quite visible. Sal said no car left the property for at least a half hour after Three-Zee left the building. However, there's no camera on the forest road, although the gate is locked, and he doesn't know how many people have a key."

"You know her best. Assuming she was merely confused and not abducted, where might she have gone?"

"That's a tough one. I say somewhere outdoors. Pete already hiked around the lake, which is pretty much her favorite trail, but I know she kind of likes that new trail we discovered that leads out toward the hunter's cabin."

"Okay, I'm going to call the detective handling this case and make a plea for a search based on her possible mental state. We can get our canine unit over here to try to track her."

"Unless she was hauled away in a car."
"Yeah, unless that, but at least we'd know one way or the other."

The Searchers

It was after five o'clock when the canine unit showed up in the employee parking lot. Even though she was officially off duty, Liz hung around to help with the search. She introduced me to Kyle Onslow, the officer coupled with Shark, a beautiful golden-colored German Shepherd.

"I'm not sure we can do much tonight anymore," Kyle said. "It'll be dark in a couple of hours, and we might have to cover quite a bit of ground unless she was taken away in a car. Of course, then Shark's usefulness ceases."

"If the trail doesn't end in the parking lot, would horses help?"

"Yeah, we could cover ground a lot faster that way, and I can ride."

"I'll call Lizzie and have her saddle four horses and meet us here with them just in case."

I glanced at Liz. "Yeah, I can ride a bit, too," she said, "although I'm not an expert."

"As long as you can stay mounted at a walk or trot, you'll be fine," I said. Then I grabbed my phone and searched for Lizzie's number while Liz and Kyle led Shark upstairs to sniff Three-Zee's pajamas. I'm not sure I'd want to have to do that for a living, but I guess dogs don't care what they sniff.

It took about ten minutes until Liz and Kyle emerged from the stairwell exit following Shark who had his nose to the ground. Another job I'd gladly leave to the dogs. Who knows what stinky stuff had passed that way? Still, dogs do run around sniffing each other's butts, so I guess they're pretty tolerant in that area.

Shark led them across the parking lot, occasionally having to skirt a parked car that probably hadn't been parked there when Three-Zee passed by. I only hoped the dog wouldn't hare off on a trail that had been made yesterday, but then I remembered Three-Zee had been in the hospital for a couple of days and had gone directly from my car into the other entrance last evening, so any earlier trail should be considerably weaker than one made last night.

Shark continued across the lot to the exit road and then continued along it to the branch that leads past our cottage—that area isn't visible to a surveillance camera, either—and onto the forest road. "It looks like he's heading for our cottage," I said. "Do you think Three-Zee might have been headed there?"

"It's possible," Liz said, "although there would be a stronger trail for her that way because she walked that every day." Kyle merely said we should wait and see, although so far it didn't appear that Three-Zee had been taken away in a car or other vehicle.

The strongest old trail would have led right up to our cottage door, but Shark didn't turn that way, continuing instead onto the forest road. While I couldn't remember exactly when Three-Zee had gone that way, I was sure she'd been in and out of the cottage since then, so Shark was probably still following last night's trail.

By now Lizzie had arrived with the horses, riding Blackie and leading Honey, Spike, and Annabelle. I decided to mount Honey, hoping we wouldn't hear any gunshots or other sharp noises, with Kyle, still holding Shark's lead, climbing onto Spike and Liz mounting Annabelle.

A dog following a scent trail often can run much faster than a person can walk or even run, so the horses gave us an advantage, especially as we wanted to cover as much ground as possible in the time we had before it became too dark to follow the track. The scent certainly would still be there, but I didn't think it would be a good idea to go trail riding in the dark. I wasn't sure how bright the moonlight would be tonight, but I vaguely remembered it as being fairly bright a couple of nights ago.

As our horses walked side by side, I said to Liz, "I can't imagine why anybody would want to kill Three-Zee. I mean, as probably her best friend or at least her longest, I've had that urge a few times, but what best friend doesn't. There was Jimmy Smits back in eleventh grade. He was hot and I was head over heels, but then Three-Zee came along, and all of a sudden she was the one and I was chopped liver. Yeah, I would gladly have strangled her then."

"So, what happened to Jimmy Smits?"

"The last time I heard, he was selling used cars and living in a run-down trailer in a derelict trailer park near Lancaster. Probably it was best neither one of us remained with him."

"No, probably not. I really never kept track of my former boyfriends, but I wouldn't be surprised if none of them turned out to be Prince Charming."

By now we had reached the point where the trail cut off the forest road and led to where we'd held the Haunted Woods event last fall and where the new dock provided a place for boats from the lake to tie up. Shark turned onto that trail and continued along it at a fairly fast pace. I was surprised he could follow a scent trail that quickly, but Kyle said the scent would be present on weeds and brush bordering the trail as well, essentially anything Three-Zee had brushed against.

When we reached the clearing where the new trailer had just arrived and was being set up, I worried that Shark would turn toward the dock where Three-Zee could have been loaded into a waiting boat and spirited away that way. However, Shark continued across the clearing and onto the lane that led out to the paved road. Then the dog turned abruptly onto the side trail that led eventually to the hunter's cabin.

"Do you know where this leads?" Kyle asked.

"Yeah, it soon leaves resort property, crosses the road that passes our dam, and continues on to a cabin in the woods. That's where we found the body of that guy." I almost said, "that guy who carjacked Lauren Capobianco," but I caught myself in time. Liz knew about that and our ability to see and talk to ghosts, although I'm not sure she really believed us, but trying to explain it to Kyle would be well above my pay grade.

"Oh yeah, I got involved with that. We used Shark to track his trail back to where that car was wrecked, so we're pretty sure he was somehow involved and was thrown from the car as it rolled down the hill."

"Mm," I said, about as non-committal as one can get. I looked around, somewhat surprised Pete hadn't joined us on our quest. However, he hadn't been with us when Kyle had shown up with Shark, so he wouldn't have known we were off tracking Three-Zee's trail. Of course, he could have been following us in his invisible state. When he's that way, I have no way of knowing he's there unless he happens to chill me.

When we got to the paved road, Shark stopped and sniffed around, looking a bit confused, but finally he managed to pick up the trail on the other side of the road. Kyle explained that cars passing by on the road probably had disturbed the scent enough that he had to search to find it again. He said the dog was trained to sniff in an expanding circle when he lost the scent so that he hopefully would pick it up again after distracting scents were passed by. In this case the continuing trail on the other side of the road made the most sense, considering that Three-Zee had been making her way in that direction and would have had no reason to turn off onto the paved road. Of course, why she was following this trail at all made little sense to me, but maybe when we found her, she'd be able to explain—if we found her.

Shark trotted fairly rapidly along the trail where we'd earlier tracked Tyrone Geiger by following footprints and blood drops, so it seemed that Three-Zee had gone at least as far as the cabin. Of course, we wouldn't know that until the dog reached that point. It was possible she'd passed out or otherwise left the trail, and it was equally possible she'd passed the cabin and continued along the access road. If she'd gone to the cabin, maybe she'd thought of something related to who might have shot Mr. Geiger or who had fired the shot that spooked Honey or even who might have been driving the black SUV we'd seen leaving the cabin. Or, maybe not.

I looked at the sky, which was rapidly clouding over. Because sunset was approaching and the clouds were thickening, it was growing darker, and I wondered whether we'd be able to find Three-Zee before it grew too dark to continue. I asked Kyle who said he had a powerful flashlight, so we could keep going as long as it didn't start to rain. Fortunately, none of the trail we'd followed was steep or dangerous, so traversing it after dark wouldn't be too difficult.

We reached the cabin without Shark leaving the trail. He went to the door and barked a couple of times. Meanwhile, the rest of us dismounted and found convenient trees to tie our horses.

I tried the doorknob, but it was locked. "Three-Zee, are you in there?" I called, but there was no reply. The window curtains were drawn shut, so it was impossible to see inside, and there was no light shining behind them.

Liz walked over to check. "Darn! We don't have a key for the place, so I guess we'll have to get a warrant to get inside. We had one during the murder investigation, but I'm not sure it's still in effect."

"But you haven't solved the murder yet, have you?" I asked. "Would the warrant expire before the investigation's complete?"

"I don't think so, but I'd have to check with the office. Kyle, do you know?"

"No, but I wasn't expecting to wind up here."

"Hm. Why don't you folks go check on the horses?" I suggested. I glanced at Lizzie, who was grinning ear to ear.

"Check on the horses…" Liz looked at me curiously. "Oh yeah, I think that would be a good idea. Also, I'm sure Shark needs a treat, doesn't he, Kyle?"

Kyle grinned. "Yeah, I'm sure he'd like one. He did a great tracking job." Both police officers turned their backs and walked to where the horses were tied, taking Shark with them. Lizzie, meanwhile, moved to a spot where she could block their view of me just in case they looked.

As soon as they were far enough away, I pulled a paper clip from my little belt pouch, straightened it, and began probing at the lock. A couple of minutes later I announced, "Gee, I guess this door wasn't locked anyway. It must have been stuck." I pushed the door open as Liz and Kyle rejoined us.

Nothing in the room appeared to have changed, but it was hard to tell because the sky had darkened so much that with the closed curtains or drapes, it was really dark inside. Liz switched on a light, but nobody other than the four of us seemed to be anywhere in the room.

We didn't find Three-Zee anywhere in the cottage. We checked everywhere, even in places where I'm sure Three-Zee wouldn't have fit. She's not a very big woman, only five-two, a little taller than me, and neither of us is overweight, but I thought it was a bit ridiculous to be looking in shelves in a linen closet that Snickers would have had a tough time hiding in.

Liz said they'd done a very thorough inspection of the place while dealing with Tyrone Geiger's body, and there were definitely no cellars or other hidden areas. The living room area ceiling went all the way up to the wood planks of the peaked roof. A storage area was over the bedrooms, but that was easily accessed from a stepstool through a door high on the living room wall. Lizzie clambered up, opened the door, and saw a few boxes, but again, nothing big enough to hold Three-Zee or any other human being except maybe an infant. I'm leaving out a body carved into parts. There are some things I don't like thinking about.

"What now?" I asked as we all gathered in the living room area.

"I can get Shark to see whether the trail continues beyond here," Kyle said. Liz switched off the light and we went outside, pulling the door shut behind us. I checked to make sure it was locked while Kyle retrieved Shark from where he was tied.

The dog returned to the door, sniffed at it a few times, and then, after Kyle directed him, headed off toward where it was possible to park a car. There the dog looked confused, sniffed around the area, and then came back to us.

"I'd say Three-Zee was here, maybe even inside the cabin at one point, and then taken away in some sort of vehicle," Kyle said.

"Oh great! So, all we have to do now is figure out who wanted to kidnap her, which is exactly what we had to do earlier."

"With no answers," Liz added. "Okay, I'm officially escalating this to a missing persons case for a person with possibly diminished capabilities. That will put it to a higher level. Let's see, we already have her fingerprints, yours too, from when you found the body, but a good DNA sample would be a big help."

"We can get that at the cottage. Her hairbrush and comb will have plenty of hair. I think that's good."

"Only if it contains roots, but a hairbrush is usually a good source of such hairs. Also, her toothbrush would work if she's been using it for a while."

"Yeah, we're both kind of slack at replacing those things." I looked up at the sky, which by now was almost dark. "I hope your flashlight batteries are good," I said. Then I walked to where Honey was tied, untied her, and climbed into the saddle. The others mounted their horses, too, and we began a slow ride back to Mountain Woods.

** ** **

I knocked on the door and waited patiently for a response. Typically, employees don't knock on their boss's apartment door at eight-thirty p.m., but in this case, George is engaged to Three-Zee's mother and has been for a while, so I figured it would be appropriate for him to be brought up to date about his future stepdaughter as soon as possible.

"Bambi, what's the latest?" George asked after he opened the door and invited me inside.

"We used a tracking dog to trace Three-Zee's movements, and he led us to that cabin in the woods where we found that dead guy."

"The one who carjacked Lauren Capobianco?"

"Yeah, that's the one."

"Was she there?"

"Three-Zee? No, it looks like she was never inside the cabin although we're not quite sure about that, but then her scent trail led to a spot just outside the cabin where a car could pull up. That's where we lost it."

"That's not good news."

"No, it isn't, but the cops are escalating their search, considering Three-Zee to be a person with diminished responsibilities."

"At this point, I'd agree."

"Have you notified Hazel yet?" Hazel Zook is Three-Zee's mother. Hazel is also my own mother's first name, but that's mere coincidence.

"I called her Monday evening right after Three-Zee was admitted to the hospital, but with Three-Zee's condition stable, Hazel called me back Tuesday morning and said she'd try to get up here this weekend. Apparently, her employer was cutting up rough about her taking off. Something about being short-staffed. However, now I plan to call her and fill her in on what's been going on. Maybe that will sway that damned store she works for. I mean, she's only a part-time cashier."

"I know, but some bosses can be real bastards. I'm not including you in that group, of course."

"Nice recovery, Bambi. I try not to be. Why don't you wait here? I'll call Hazel now and put her on speaker."

"Yeah, good idea."

As a result of the call, Hazel said she was going to call the store manager—she had his home number—and give him an ultimatum. Give her a few days off without pay to go to Mountain Woods to learn more about her daughter's disappearance or hire someone to replace her. Hazel was pretty sure her boss wouldn't fire her because he was already short-staffed, and he wouldn't be able to replace her easily. We wished her luck—George even offered her a job at the resort—but she said she really didn't want to leave the farm just yet. Of course, that would change when she and George married, but they hadn't set any sort of date yet.

After we disconnected, I asked, "Do you have any ideas as to what we can do to look for her?"

"Bambi, you know her better than anybody else, probably even better than her mother does. If you don't have any ideas, what makes you think I would?"

"I don't know. I guess I'm just grasping at straws. If she'd only managed to take her phone…"

"Yes, nowadays that's always an issue. When I was a kid, we didn't have phones we could carry in our pockets, but I admit they often come in handy."

"Well, I hope she's still alive and that the smotherer didn't decide to carry out his original plan."

"Couldn't it have been a woman?"

"Yes, it could have been, actually. Almost anybody except a little kid. Unfortunately, we've been dealing with too many security cameras that are out of order or are aimed in the wrong direction or videos that don't give clear enough images."

"You haven't seen her ghost, have you?"

"No, fortunately, although we don't always see people's ghosts, even though they died nearby. We haven't seen Tyrone Geiger's ghost yet."

"Tyrone… oh yeah, the carjacker. I guess you couldn't see everybody's ghosts before they moved on. Otherwise, you'd be overwhelmed."

"True. Can you imagine being an undertaker and seeing the ghost of everybody you had to prepare for their funeral?"

"No, but at least you'd be able to honor their last wishes."

"Yeah, but try to convince their families."

In the Dark

I'm pretty sure I'm lying on a floor. At least it feels like carpet or a rug or something. I must have just woken up.

This whole thing isn't going according to plan. It seemed right at the time to get out of bed, pull on my clothes, and then go out looking for clues. That cabin in the woods doesn't make sense. I mean, why would a carjacker who'd just been thrown from a tumbling vehicle, probably saving his life, run off into the woods, find an empty cabin, somehow get inside, and then be shot to death? Who was the shooter? The owner, maybe? That would be the most likely option. However, why would the owner leave the body lying in the middle of the floor, definitely making himself or herself the most likely suspect for the murder?

I'd awakened at around midnight and wasn't able to get back to sleep, so I had crawled out of bed, pulled on my clothes, put on a jacket, and left the room. Of course, the hallway is always lit, I used the stairs to avoid having the elevator make noise and the stairwell is lit, and I went outside, and crossed the parking lot, all lit. It wasn't until I was on the roadway that leads past our cottage that I realized I hadn't brought my phone, so I had no light from there on.

I don't think my brain was firing on all cylinders—heck, I'm not sure it is now—so instead of turning back to get the phone or behave more rationally, I continued past the cottage—no point in disturbing Bambi, plus I didn't have my key so I couldn't let myself in—and onto the forest road. I've walked that road so many times, I probably could do it in total darkness. However, there was enough moonlight—not full, but more than half—that I could make my way very well. I admit that I nearly turned back when I passed the Haunted Woods area because I wasn't really all that comfortable with the route after that, but there was enough light that I could walk carefully and more-or-less not fall over something and break my neck.

I remember when I left the employee housing building that somebody had been behind me when I went down the stairs and followed me outside, but apparently, they weren't really following me; just going about their business. Anyway, I didn't notice anybody following me after I passed our cottage. That doesn't mean somebody wasn't. It just means I don't think I was paying much attention.

Damned fuzzy brain. I don't think I've recovered completely from that concussion. Also, my head still aches.

I remember reaching the cabin and trying the door, but it was locked. Without Bambi's lockpicking skills—I really must take the time to have her teach me—I was stuck. I could search around the outside of the cabin, of course, but I doubted that would tell me anything I didn't already know. Of course, there was that black SUV, but there didn't seem to be any of those—in fact, no vehicles of any kind—anywhere in sight.

Okay, maybe I was wrong about nobody following me. I mean, how would anybody have known I'd be snooping around the cabin at—What was it?—two in the morning or thereabouts. Without my phone I had no idea of the time. Of course, even with the phone I wouldn't have been able to call for help because the cabin's in one of those annoying dead spots. Maybe someday you'll be able to use your phone anywhere in the country, but that day isn't here yet.

I don't like being grabbed from behind, but then I suspect nobody does. That's what happened, though. The grabber put something over my face that had a weird smell.

Where I am now, I'm not sure. It's really dark and quiet. At least it's not cold or wet, but I'm pretty sure I'm inside something—a building or a room, but definitely not a big cardboard box like at Ocean City. This has happened before, of course, but in every case, I had a pretty good idea of where I was. This time, not a clue. I mean, a carpeted floor could be nearly anywhere. People put that indoor/outdoor carpeting on their patios, too, but I'm sure I'd either feel a chill or a breeze or something if I were outdoors. It's the end of April—not exactly summer yet.

I kind of think I'm still alive, but I could be dead, a ghost, and in my invisible state. Or maybe I've already moved on, and this is what eternity will be like. If it is, I'll tell you right now, I don't like it.

I've considered yelling for help, but I'm not sure that would do any good. For one thing, I don't think there's anybody around, although I thought that earlier and look how that turned out. I could maybe go back to sleep. This probably is nothing more than a bad dream, and when I wake up the sun will be shining, the birds will be singing, and all will be right with the world. Or maybe not.

Unfortunately, I really have to pee. Can you feel that way while you're dreaming? Come to think of it, having to pee is probably a good thing because I doubt ghosts ever have to pee—Why would they?—so that means I'm still alive. I don't seem to be shackled or tied up in any way, so what's stopping me from finding a bathroom. Oh yeah, it's pitch dark, and I have no idea where I might find a bathroom, and I have a really bad headache.

Okay, first things first, Three-Zee.

Sit up.

Good.

Now, get to your feet.

Okay, managed that, but the floor seems to be swaying. Maybe I'm just dizzy. Yeah, a dizzy brunette.

Now, extend your arms in front of you and walk slowly forward until you reach a wall or other obstruction.

Hm, what if there's a drop-off in front of me?

Okay, slide right foot forward testing for missing floor.

Nope, no missing floor.

Now, shift weight to right foot and slide left foot forward past right foot, testing again for missing floor.

Okay, now keep doing that, still testing with outstretched hands for wall.

Whoops! Bumped into something with right leg.

What the heck? It's a bed. That pretty much guarantees I'm inside a room somewhere.

Maneuver around bed.

Okay, past bed. Wall ahead.

Start walking along wall.

Opening; feels like doorway.

Through opening.

Ow! Something hard.

Oh, it's a toilet.

Ah, relief.

Okay, what the heck am I doing in a totally dark bedroom with attached bathroom?

I'm pretty sure I'm not dreaming, but where am I?

Hm. A place like this should have electricity. If I feel around here by the door, I should be able to find a light switch. Yeah, there it is.

Funny. The switch works but the light doesn't come on. Okay, bulb burned out or power off.

Back out into room. Turn left along wall.

Sharp turn.

Another door. This one won't open. Odd.

Headache getting worse.

Where's that bed?

Ooof! Found it. Fell onto it.

Still dark. Must sleep.

Looking for the Lost

I was up early on Friday morning. I took care of Snickers' needs, showered, dressed, and headed for George's apartment. He was up and dressed, too, and said Hazel Zook had called him at five-thirty, said she'd spoken with her supervisor last evening, and was leaving for the resort in a few minutes.

I was ready to leave for the kitchen to start my shift when somebody knocked on George's door. It was too early for Hazel to have arrived—she would have had to speed all the way—but I was surprised to see Sal Aviedo standing there.

"What's up, Sal?" I asked. "Isn't this a bit early for you?"

"Is George here?"

"I'm here," George called. "Come on in."

Once inside, Sal said, "I saw something on the surveillance video that may or may not be important."

"Which video?" George asked.

The one looking out over the guest parking lot from the front portico—the one looking toward the south entrance."

"Okay, what did you see?"

"The recording was from about four a.m. yesterday morning. I had checked all the other camera recordings, but I really didn't think this would show anything, which is why I left it for last. Anyway, a big black SUV pulled up outside the south entrance and pulled into a parking space almost next to it. A man got out of the driver's side, closed that door, and walked around to the passenger side. He opened that door and helped what looked like a young woman out of the car. Then he helped her walk to the entrance door—she was either very drunk or very sick—opened the door with his key card, and led her inside."

"Yeah, well, that's maybe a bit reprehensible, but it's not exactly illegal as long as the woman was an adult. Heck, it could even have been the man's wife. Could you see who either of them were?"

"Stuff like that happens all the time, spouse or not, but what makes this interesting is that the man certainly looked a lot like Mr. Pendergast. Also, I checked his key activity, and it was used to open that door then, access five on the elevator about a minute later, and his suite a few minutes after that."

"Marvelous Marvin? Er, forget I called him that. I can't imagine him sneaking a floozy into his room. Heck, I'm not sure he'd know what do to with her if her got her there. Okay, I never said that, either."

Sal was grinning from ear to ear by now.

"Did you happen to see who the young woman was?" I asked.

"No, it was too far away to get a really good image. In night mode, the image is never as clear as it is in the daytime. I switched to the camera inside the south entry, but it seems to be out of order as is the one in the hallway on five. I'll notify maintenance as soon as I leave here. All of the cameras should be working. It's bad enough that the one on Three-Zee's floor here in employee housing isn't working."

"Can we see the video?" George asked.

"Sure. Come on down to the security office and I'll run it for you."

I glanced at George. "I guess I should get down to the kitchen."

"Wait a minute. I'll call, and you can go with us. You'd be able to recognize Three-Zee better that we would." George picked up the phone, punched in a number, and told somebody, maybe Fred, that I'd be a bit late. Then we followed Sal to the security office.

** ** **

"Thank heavens the resort opted for motion-sensitive equipment when they installed this latest security system," Sal said as he pressed button images on the screen. "Scrolling through hours of real-time recordings is darned near impossible. By the time you've found what you're looking for, you're either half asleep or bored out of your skull. With motion-sensitive you do still have a lot of footage during busy times of the day, but night surveillance, which is often what you're searching, goes rather quickly, and it's still date and time stamped for legal reference." He touched a few more button images. "Here's what I saw."

George and I watched as a black SUV, or at least dark-colored because colors are difficult to determine in night-vision mode, pulled into an empty parking space near the south entrance. The time stamp showed four-oh-two a.m. The driver's side door, which was on the camera side, opened and a short, skinny man got out. "That sure as hell looks like Marvin," George said.

The man walked around to the other side of the vehicle, opened the door, and helped a person get out. When they walked past the front of the car, the person definitely looked like a woman no taller than Marvin. She was leaning on him and obviously having a great deal of difficulty walking. I had Sal rerun the sequence from the time the woman got out of the SUV until the two of them, she still leaning on Marvin for support, entered the south entrance.

"It's Three-Zee," I said. "I'm sure it's Three-Zee."

"How can you be sure?" George asked. "You can't see her face or hair style, and she's not walking normally so you can't tell from that."

"It's true that Three-Zee is rarely that drunk, and when I've seen her like that, I'm usually in the same condition, but it's just the way she carries herself. Besides, how the heck would Marvelous Marvin be able to coax a woman to his room without getting her drunk first?"

"Good point," George said, "and I don't disagree with you, but do we have enough to go busting into Marvin's suite and searching it?"

"I don't know. However, I'm calling Liz Heyer right now. Maybe they can come up with something."

"Yeah, well, one of the rules about hotels is that management can search a guest's room if they believe something illegal or even something against hotel rules is going on. I don't actually need a search warrant for that. However, the cops would still need a search warrant if they conduct the search."

"What about the fact that Marvin is part owner?"

"That kind of complicates things a bit, but technically he's not manager. I am."

"Mm. But it wouldn't hurt if Liz knew about our suspicions."

"No, not at all. She at least could watch the surveillance video because that's video of a public area. All of our surveillance videos meet that criterion. However, she couldn't go crashing into a guest room without a warrant."

"Which she'd have to get from a judge."

"Yes, and describing the specific reason for the search."

"Such as looking for a victim of kidnapping with pretty good suspicion the rooms being searched contain that victim."

"Yes, probably such as that."

** ** **

Liz came over as soon as she could, accompanied by a member of the detective bureau. Together they watched the selected videos: those of Three-Zee leaving the building, and her possible return in what appeared to be a drunken state. "Although it's possible her concussion is acting up again, or maybe she's been drugged," I suggested.

"Yes, I agree it does look like her," Liz said, "especially because what she's wearing in the clear videos when she left the building seems to be what the woman is wearing while being helped into the building by Mr. Pendergast. It's unfortunate that the cameras at that entry and in the hallways are out of order. I'd suggest you get them fixed as soon as possible."

"Definitely high on my list of things to have done," George said. "Maintenance is already looking into it." He turned to me. "Bambi, I know Fred will probably be on his high horse about you not showing up for your shift in the kitchen, but I already called and left a message that you have my permission to take off. You may have to skip a day off sometime in the future, though."

"That's okay. If you can't be there for your best friend, what good is friendship?"

Light and Fuzzy

This bed is so comfortable. I could just lie here forever or at least for a couple more hours. Still, I guess they wouldn't like it if I peed in it, so I'd better find that bathroom again. Darn! I'm hungry, too. I wonder how long it's been since I had anything to eat. Not eating is a tough way to diet.

Mm. Wait. I can actually see some light. Are my eyes open. Yeah, now they are. Everything's fuzzy, really blurry, but at least it's no longer completely dark. Maybe they fixed the lights while I was sleeping. Still, why would somebody come in, fix the lights, and leave again without waking me?

Let's see. I can sort of make out an open doorway over there and the light is coming from inside whatever room that is. I sort of remember that the bathroom was in that direction, so that's probably it. Yeah, that's right, I did switch on the bathroom light, but at the time it didn't come on. I'll just get to my feet and—Whoa! What the heck was I drinking last night?—no, maybe it's from that darned concussion they said I had. I guess you can have relapses from those things. I'm not sure. I'll have to ask Bambi. She knows all that scientific stuff.

Speaking of Bambi, I wonder where she is. Come to think of it, I wonder where I am. Darned headache. I wish somebody was around with an aspirin, a giant aspirin about the size of a jumbo pizza. That might help.

Okay, the room with the light is the bathroom, and I just made it in time although I nearly fell. It's good that doorframe was there for me to grab.

Mm. Feel a lot better, at least in the bladder department, but my head still hurts. A lot. Okay, I think I can make it back to bed. At least when I'm asleep I don't notice the headache.

Confrontation

"Liz, is there any law against me going up there and confronting Marvin?" I asked.

"Well, no, not really. If you physically assault him, of course, that's a totally different thing, but merely knocking on his door and then yelling at him from the public hallway if he decides to open it isn't exactly illegal. I'm not even sure he could sue you for it, but he'd be within his rights to slam the door in your face. He could also ask Mr. Wylie to fire you, but doing so would then be up to Mr. Wylie. I assume Marvin doesn't have a controlling interest."

George shook his head. "No, only around thirty-five percent. I guess he could get a couple of other investors on his side to make up more than fifty percent, but I'm not sure anybody on the board likes him enough to join up with him in a case like that. Actually, I suspect most of the board members would like to knock on his door and yell at him themselves. I know I would."

"And you don't do it because…"

"It would be beneath my dignity as a hotel manager."

Liz laughed. "Okay, I can accept that." She looked at me. "Bambi, why are you standing here?"

"What do you mean?"

"I'd have thought that by now you'd be upstairs pounding on Marvelous Marvin's door. Remember, I'm only conjecturing, not suggesting."

"Yeah, I understand. I'm off to the elevator. If you need me, I'll be soaking my sore fist."

"Not from hitting Marvin, I hope."

"No, he's not worth hitting, but those doors are really hard."

"Er, Bambi, you won't be able to get to his floor using the elevator. That level requires key card access."

"Darn! No, damn!"

Sal put out his hand. "Give me your key card for a moment. I think you're in the system incorrectly." He took it, looked at the number on the card, and then typed a few things into a computer. "Okay, you're up to date."

"Gee, thanks, Sal," I said as I took the card from his hand. Sal, George, and Liz all grinned. The detective with Liz—I never did get his name—looked a bit confused, but then I doubted he'd ever met Marvin.

As I left the security office, I heard Sal say, "Darn, I think I just accidentally gave her access to the bridal suite. Oh well, I can fix it later. Now I must get started on my rounds."

** ** **

Marvin did open his door to my pounding, probably thinking I was from housekeeping, although that staff is required to announce, "Housekeeping," when they knock. He stared at me, probably not recognizing me, but then I'm not sure we ever had been face to face.

"Where is she?" I snapped.

"Where is who?" Marvin looked shocked, but I guess that would be a normal reaction regardless of what he'd done.

"Three-Zee."

"Who the hell is Three-Zee?" Now he looked merely angry.

"The girl you're hiding somewhere in there."

"What makes you think I'm hiding a girl in here?" Still angry.

"I saw you bring her in, obviously either drunk, drugged, or sick."

"Who the hell are you, anyway?" More pissed off, if that was possible.

"Bambi Bamberger."

"And this Three-Zee is…?"

"My best friend, who's been suffering from concussion. I'm worried you probably killed her and are hiding her body in one of your rooms."

"I what? Lady, you're crazy. I'm calling security. How the hell did you get on this floor, anyway? It's restricted access."

"None of your business. Anyway, you haven't answered my question."

"Which question?"

"Where the hell is Three-Zee?"

Before Marvin could answer I heard a male voice from somewhere behind him say, "What's going on, Marv?" That voice sounded vaguely familiar.

"Nothing," Marvin muttered. Then he turned around as the source of the voice came into view.

"Luke Skywalker," I said, probably as surprised to see him as Marvin had been to see me, "what the heck are you doing here?"

"It's Luke Walker. Hey, ain't you that babe who was hanging out with Three-Zee the other day?"

"Yeah, I'm Bambi, but I'm not a babe."

"Oh, I don't know. You're pretty hot looking to me."

"Shut up, Walker!" Marvin snapped. "And remember, you don't know anything."

True to his name, Walker walked up to me, grabbed my shoulder, pulled me into the room, and then pushed the door shut with his foot. It all happened so quickly, I didn't have time to react.

"So, where's Three-Zee?" I asked again after Luke had let me go.

"Oh, she's still alive," he said.

"I said, 'Shut up!' "Marvin snapped.

"Hey, Marv, I think it's kind of late for that now that we've got both of them on our hands." Luke looked at me. "Who else knows you're up here?"

For a moment I considered answering, "Nobody," but then I realized that my life, and Three-Zee's, too, might depend upon them realizing others did know. "The cops are downstairs with George. They know I'm here."

Marvin muttered something that sounded suspiciously like a four-letter word for human excrement. "This is your fault," he added, looking directly at Luke as he said it.

"My fault? What do you mean, my fault?"

"If you hadn't botched that job at the hospital the other night..."

"Okay, I wasn't expecting her to wake up. Besides, you never did explain why you wanted her dead."

For a moment I wondered whether they'd completely forgotten I was there. Unfortunately, they hadn't. "You," Marvin snapped, which seemed to be his usual method of addressing people, "come over here." By now he was standing on the far side of the living room next to one of the doors that, I assumed, led into a bedroom.

"Like I said, plenty of people know I'm here."

"Yeah, like you said, so we'll have to deal with that."

"And if I refuse to come over there."

"You probably shouldn't," Luke said. I turned my head to see a small, but probably highly effective, handgun in his, okay, hand, and it was pointed directly at me. "In case you haven't heard, I'm a crack shot."

"You probably should listen to him," a voice on the other side of me said. These voices were becoming a bit unnerving. I spun to my left, never considering that such an action might make Luke Walker's itchy trigger finger suddenly contract. Pete was standing there. "Three-Zee's in that room. She looks unharmed, but she's asleep, I think. Anyway, I'm sure she's not dead or I'd know it."

I turned back to see both Marvin and Luke staring at me. "What the heck was that all about?" Marvin asked.

"Yeah, you don't have to practice your dance steps," Luke added.

"Oh, nothing. I thought I heard something from the hall."

"So, get your sorry butt in gear and get over there," Luke said, waving the gun. I've never quite figured out why people holding someone at gunpoint start waving the gun. Surely that would mess up their aim should they decide to pull the trigger.

Luke stepped back away from me and toward where Marvin was standing. I had my hand in my pocket from putting my key card in there, and for some reason I had never pulled it out. However, I felt something crinkly, and I realized I'd stuffed a wrapper into my pocket from a treat I'd given Snickers this morning. I crumpled the wrapper and casually removed my hand from my pocket clutching it. Then I dropped it to the floor behind me. I hoped the mostly clear cellophane or plastic or whatever wouldn't be too noticeable lying on the carpet, at least not noticeable to Marvin and Luke who by now were a good ten feet away. As I did it, I said, " 'Sorry butt?' So much for 'hot babe.' "

"Okay, you're still a hot babe, if that makes you happy. You're just not my kind of hot babe."

"Thank the good Lord," I muttered as Marvin opened the door into the bedroom and ushered me inside. The bedroom light was off, but there was enough light from the bathroom and leaking around the window drapes that I could see someone lying on the bed. Marvin slammed the door behind me, and the person on the bed moved a bit.

"Three-Zee?" I ran to the bed and switched on a reading light on a bedside table.

"Er, yeah, I think it's me."

"It's definitely you. Are you okay?"

"Define 'okay.' If you mean, not feeling any pain from a bleeding wound, yeah. However, if you include killer headache and equally killer hunger pangs, then not okay."

"Hunger we can deal with as soon as we get you out of here, and probably the headache, too."

Three-Zee raised her head from the pillow and looked around as well as she could before dropping it again and grunting. Then she said, "Who's we?"

"George, Liz, some detective, Sal, Pete."

"Where are they?"

"Well, Pete's out there with Marvin and Luke, and the others are downstairs, but they all know I'm up here."

"Marvin? Luke? Are they good guys? I never had Marvin figured for one of those."

"No, those two are definitely bad guys. I'm not sure why they brought you here, but they did."

"Where's here?"

"Marvin's suite—the bridal suite."

"Hell, I'm not his bride, am I?"

"I sure as hell hope not. However, I think a marriage performed when one of the parties is under duress isn't valid."

"Still, it would be kind of neat. I could inherit his share of the resort."

"He'd have to croak first."

"Oh yeah, and that probably isn't likely, at least not in the immediate future."

"No, probably not."

"I'm not dead, am I. After all, you can see and talk to ghosts, so I could be dead, and you might not know it."

"No, Pete checked on you earlier and said you were asleep but definitely not dead."

"Good. I don't think I want to be dead. Eventually, like a long time in the future, but not now. But if this headache keeps up…"

I tried the door into the living room, but somehow it was locked. That seemed odd to me. People lock bedroom doors to keep others out, not lock them to keep people in. However, there was no lock button on my side of the door. I put my ear to the door, but it was thick enough that all I heard were faint voices, raised, but too faint to make out words. I was pretty sure at least one of our captors was yelling at the other.

Pete came walking through a wall. "They're not happy with each other," he said.

"I sort of gathered that considering they seem to be yelling at each other."

"Yeah, they are. Something about Luke being trigger-happy, but I don't understand the reason."

"Have you seen George and the others?"

"No, and I have no way of telling them you're in trouble. However, maybe at least one of them is one their way up here. I'll go check." Pete walked through the wall again, disappearing into the living room. I went to the window and pulled open the drapes. It was going to be a nice, sunny day, but I wondered whether we'd be able to enjoy it.

** ** **

I pulled a chair to the bedside and sat, while Three-Zee lay on the bed and closed her eyes. "My head hurts worse when I have my eyes open," she said.

"Should I close the drape again and turn off the bathroom light? You might feel better if it's dark."

"No, if this is where it all ends, I at least want to go out in the sunshine."

Just then the voices outside the door grew louder, and then I heard what sounded suspiciously like a gunshot. I dived onto the bed and tried my best to cover Three-Zee with my own body although I doubted I'd be much help in blocking a bullet.

There was more shouting and then the bedroom door crashed open. I closed my eyes and gritted my teeth. Was this the end? I remembered an old Peggy Lee song my mother used to play, 'Is that all there is?' "

"Bambi, Three-Zee, are you okay?" George's voice.

I rolled off Three-Zee and sat up. "Yeah, I think we're okay. Three-Zee?"

"No sharp pains, so I think the bullets missed."

"What just happened out there?" I asked.

"I opened the suite door with my key—I do have that right if I suspect something's wrong—and that Walker kid and Marvin were standing there staring at me. You must have been in here by then because when I asked whether they'd seen you, they said they hadn't. Then, I spotted that wrapper on the floor. I really thought housekeeping might have missed it, so I bent over and picked it up. I realized what it was, a Friskies wrapper, and I was pretty sure Marvin wasn't nibbling on cat treats—he'd be too cheap to buy them—so I asked him if he had a cat in here, and he said he hates the damned things. That was when I was pretty sure you had been here and dropped the wrapper.

"Then, that Walker kid aimed a gun at me. Liz and that detective guy with her were standing just outside in the hall, so when somebody points a gun at me, and that gun sort of is aimed at them, too, they are allowed to defend themselves. Liz shot the gun out of Walker's hand before he could pull the trigger—I don't think he saw them behind me. I have to hand it to her. That was one hell of a shot."

"Is Walker alive?"

"Yeah, but I don't think he'll be using that hand for a while. I'm pretty sure it was at least broken."

"And they're both in custody?" Three-Zee asked.

"Yeah, both of them. I'm not sure exactly what's been going on, but I suspect there's going to be some serious questioning. Was Marvin being held captive, too?"

"No, he was the boss of whatever they were up to. Luke did admit to trying to smother Three-Zee in the hospital, but beyond that, I don't know."

The Party's Over

I'm back and mostly lucid although another day in the hospital was necessary for the headache from hell to be conquered. I guess the brain swelling caused by my concussion had recurred, and that had all kinds of side effects. Bambi said I should appreciate a swelled brain because it's the smartest I'll ever be. She probably saved my life, so I should be nice to her, but I did stick out my tongue at her when she said it.

Among the side effects I suffered were dizziness, which is quite common; short-term blindness, which is very rare but, naturally, I'd be the one to suffer it; blurred vision, fairly common; and confusion, which Bambi said is my normal state. I'm still working on ways to get even with her for that. The time will come.

Liz and that detective guy—I never heard his name, either—were allowed to defend themselves when Luke Walker pulled a gun on them even though it was indirectly, so they hadn't violated the warrant laws, and George was within his rights to open the door when he suspected something illegal might be going on. Of course, the police had no problem then obtaining a search warrant, and even though a New York lawyer showed up quickly to defend Marvin, he lost most of his argument when Luke decided to come clean. That was rather odd, I thought, because he was the one who'd shot Tyrone Geiger in the cabin although Luke claimed it was self-defense.

Why was Luke at the cabin? It turned out Marvin was part owner of the cabin through some sort of hunting club of which he was a member. However, he used it more than the other members and often came to stay there to spy on what was happening at Mountain Woods without George knowing he was in the neighborhood. Marvin had tried to throw Luke to the wolves by saying he had no idea what Luke was up to and that nobody should believe Bambi, so Luke turned on him and said Marvin had a large stash of cocaine, crystal meth, and heroine in the cabin the day Tyrone Geiger showed up at the door, drugs waiting to be picked up by a local dealer. Geiger was barely conscious at that point having lost a lot of blood, but Luke was afraid he'd recover and tell somebody what he'd seen. He shot Geiger execution style, and then hid the drugs in the trunk of his car until the dealer arrived. However, he hadn't gotten around to hauling the body away—the trunk of his car was full of drugs—before Bambi and I showed up.

The day we arrived on horseback he'd been there checking to see what the police had done to the place. He saw us at a distance from a window, ran out to Marvin's car, which he was driving that day, drove a short distance up the access lane to where he was just out of sight of the cabin, and then fired a shot into the air to scare us off, figuring we'd think hunters were in the area and not want to get in the way of their bullets. He did scare Honey, of course, but Lizzie was now working on her training so she would no longer spook at loud noises.

It had been Luke behind me on the stairs the night I went walkabout, following me after being unable to open my locked room door. At that point he'd given up on smothering me, at least not there, but he wanted to find out what I was up to. Also, he had a small bottle of chloroform in his pocket to knock me out so he could search my room. When I got to the cabin, he worried I was getting too close to things, so he dumped the chloroform on his hankie and put that over my nose and mouth to put me under quickly. Then he walked another hundred yards or so where he knew he could get a cell signal and called Marvin to come get me. They decided to take me to Marvin's suite where they could decide how to get rid of me. Marvin had dropped Luke off at home on his way back to the resort, so Luke could show up at work in the morning at his usual time and say he'd been at home all night.

After Marvin had led me into his spare bedroom—it's a big suite— I'd passed out on the floor, and skinny Marvin hadn't had the strength to pick me up again, so he'd let me lie there. However, after he left me in the room, he worried that I'd recover and try to escape, so he used a screwdriver from a kit he carried to remove the doorknobs and swap them, thereby moving the lock button to the outside rather than the inside. That way he could keep me locked in.

We never did find out why Tyrone Geiger was in the area or why he'd carjacked Lauren and Johnny Capobianco with disastrous results for so many people. For some reason, his ghost never appeared to me, Bambi, Lauren, or Pete, so I guess it's possible it's still hanging around somewhere.

Harry was able to salvage his job at Mountain Woods by stating unequivocally that he had no idea what his younger brother had been up to and that he'd had little contact with Luke for a couple of years. Luke concurred with that although George did have to really think about keeping Harry on. However, Harry was a valuable employee, always did his work well, and never was in trouble in any other way, all of which combined to save his bacon or at least his job.

Luke fingered the local drug dealer, who was already on the police radar, and that worthy fingered Marvin as his supplier. Marvin tried to weasel out of it, but some really good investigative work by the Pennsylvania State Police working with other police departments and agencies got him arrested for that as well as for plotting to kill me. It never ceases to amaze me how many drug dealers inhabit a bucolic, relatively sparsely settled area like the Pocono Mountains, but they seem to be everywhere. We'd certainly had our share hanging around and even working at Mountain Woods.

I had asked Liz about whether they thought Papa Guido had been involved with Marvin's drug business, but she said it was very doubtful. Apparently, mob families are very territorial, so Papa Guido would have been well outside his territory in the Pocono Mountains, that area being controlled by a family in the Wilkes-Barre–Scranton area.

When the Pennsylvania Liquor Control Board threatened to suspend the resort's license because of Marvin's indictment, Marvin decided to sell his share, so the other owners managed to get loans and redivide the ownership. Interestingly, that left George with the majority holding although not quite control.

Mom showed up around an hour after the showdown in the bridal suite—hm, that might make a good movie title, especially for a Western—which was just as well. However, that gave her an excuse to visit George for a few days before heading back to the farm. She's an adult; I don't judge.

** ** **

We gathered in George's apartment the evening before Mom was planning to go home.

"So, when are we likely to hear wedding bells?" I asked.

George grinned, but Mom gave me a dirty look. "For your wedding?" she asked me.

"No, of course not. I'm not engaged to anybody."

"I thought by now you and that cop from Cape Cod might be planning something."

"Nothing yet although I did video chat with him last night."

"Yeah, young people and their online orgies."

"Hey, at least you can't get knocked up that way. No, I'm asking about you and George. After all, you're the ones currently cohabiting."

"Well, as you so crudely put it, I'm probably past the age of getting knocked up, but we haven't decided on anything yet." She looked at George who looked a bit flustered. I suppose it wasn't fair of me to put them on the spot like that, but it was fun, kind of.

"At least nobody's trying to get *me* married off," Bambi said.

As the only person in the room besides Bambi who could see him, I looked at Pete. He merely smiled.